GUARDIANS
OF GA'HOOLE

Journey

Broken Talon Point

Northern Kingdoms

Peninsula
of the
Spirit Woods

Ice
Narrows

Sea of Hoolemere

Cape
Glaux

Island of the
Great Ga'Hoole Tree

The Beaks

Desert
of
Kuneer

Forest Kingdom
of Tyto

Soren's Hollow

River Hoole

The Guardians of Ga'Hoole Series:

GUARDIANS
OF GA'HOOLE

BOOK TWO

The Journey

Kathryn Lasky

First published in the USA by Scholastic Inc 2003
First published in Great Britain by HarperCollins *Children's Books* 2006
HarperCollins *Children's Books* is a division of HarperCollins*Publishers* Ltd
77-85 Fulham Palace Road, Hammersmith, London W6 8JB

The HarperCollins *Children's Books* website address is
www.harpercollins.co.uk

Text copyright © Kathryn Lasky 2003
Illustrations copyright © Richard Cowdrey 2003

The author and illustrator assert the moral right to be identified as the author
and illustrator of this work

ISBN-13 978-0-00-721518-8

Find out more about HarperCollins and the environment at
www.harpercollins.co.uk/green

To Max, who imagines universes

...the four owls looked below and saw the vast sea
glinting with silver spangles from the moon's light
and then, directly ahead, spreading into the
night, were the twisting branches of the largest
tree they had ever seen, the Great Ga'Hoole Tree...

CHAPTER ONE

A Mobbing of Crows

Soren felt the blind snake shift in the deep feathers between his shoulders as he and the three other owls flew through the buffeting winds. They had been flying for hours now and it seemed as if in the last minutes the darkness had begun to dissolve drop by drop, and they were now passing from the full black of the night into the first light of the morning. Beneath them a river slid like a dark ribbon over the earth.

"Let's keep flying even though it's getting light," said Twilight, the immense Great Grey Owl who flew downwind of Soren. "We're getting nearer. I just feel it."

It was to the Sea of Hoolemere they flew, and in the middle of that sea was an island and on that island there was a tree called the Great Ga'Hoole Tree and in this tree there was an order of owls. It was said that these owls would rise each night into the blackness and perform noble deeds. The universe of owls was desperately in need of such deeds. For with its many kingdoms it was about to be destroyed by a terrible evil.

Hidden away in a maze of stone canyons and ravines there was a violent nation of deadly owls known as St Aegolius. The evil of St Aggie's, as it was often called, had touched almost every owl kingdom in some way or another. Soren and his best friend Gylfie, the tiny Elf Owl, had both been captured by St Aggie's patrols when they were young nestlings unable to fly. Twilight too had been snatched but, unlike Soren and Gylfie, he had managed to escape before being imprisoned. Digger's youngest brother had been eaten by a St Aggie's patrol and his parents later killed. Soren and Gylfie had met Twilight and Digger, a Burrowing Owl, shortly after their own daring escape from the stone canyons of St Aggie's.

Although the four owls had met as orphans, they had become so much more. In a desert still stained with the blood of two of the fiercest of St Aggie's elite warrior owls, whom they had defeated, they had discovered a knowledge, along with a feeling deep in their gizzards, where all owls felt their strongest emotions. And this knowledge was that they were a band for evermore, one for all and all for one, bound by the deepest loyalty and dedicated to the survival of the kingdoms of all owls. They had sworn an oath in that desert drenched with blood and tinged with the silver light of the moon. They would go to Hoolemere. It was as a band that they knew they must go and find its great tree, which loomed now as the heart of wisdom and nobility in a world that was becoming insane and ignoble. They must warn of the evil that threatened. They must become part of this ancient kingdom of guardian knights on silent wings.

They hoped they were drawing near even though the river they now followed was not the River Hoole, the one that led to Hoolemere. Still, Twilight said he was sure that this river would lead to the Hoole and on to Hoolemere, and the very thought of this legendary island in the sea made the four owls stroke even harder against the confusing winds. But Soren felt Mrs Plithiver stir again in his feathers. Mrs P, as he called her, had been the old nest-maid in the hollow where Soren's parents had made their home. These blind snakes had been born without eyes, and where their eyes should have been there were only two slight indentations. The rosy-scaled reptiles were kept by many owls to tend the nests and make sure they were clean and free of maggots and various vermin that found their way into the hollows. Soren had thought that he would never see Mrs P again, and yet they had found each other just days after his escape from St Aggie's. She had told him what Soren had long suspected – that it was his older brother, Kludd, who had pushed him from the nest when his parents were out hunting. Although he had survived the fall, still being flightless he was prey to any ground animal. Ground animal! Who would have ever thought another owl would be the greatest danger? Until that moment when he was snatched and felt himself being carried into the night sky by a pair of talons, Soren had thought that the worst predator in the forest, from an owl's point of view, was a raccoon. And then Mrs P told him that she suspected Kludd had done the same thing to Eglantine, his baby sister. When Mrs P had protested, Kludd had threatened to eat her. So the poor old snake had no choice but to leave – very quickly.

Now Mrs P slithered towards Soren's left ear, the higher ear and the easiest for her to reach. "Soren," she whispered, "I'm not sure if it is a good idea to keep flying with all this light. We don't want to get mobbed."

"Mobbed?" Soren asked.

"You know, crows."

Soren felt a chill run through his gizzard.

Perhaps if Mrs Plithiver had not been whispering her warning in his ear he might have heard the chuffing sound of wings, and not owl wings, overhead.

"Crow to windward!" Gylfie cried. And then suddenly the rosy dawn sky turned black.

"We're being mobbed!" shrieked Twilight.

Oh Glaux! thought Soren. This was the worst thing that could befall any owl flying in the daytime. But it was still very early. Crows at night were fine. Owls were crows' worst enemies at night. They could attack them as they slept, but crows during the day were something else. Crows in daylight were terrible. If a crow discovered an owl during the daytime, even if it was just one crow, that bird had a way of signalling others and soon an entire flock would arrive and mob the owls, diving at their heads with their sharp beaks, trying to tear out their eyes.

"Scatter!" Gylfie cried out. "Scatter and loop."

Suddenly, Gylfie seemed to be everywhere at once. She was like a crazed insect, zipping through the air. Soren, Digger and Twilight began to follow her lead. Soren quickly noticed that Gylfie would swoop up from her loops and spiralling dives to just beneath the crows, stabbing them on the underside of their wings. This made the crows drop their wings down close to their bodies and lose altitude.

"I feel one coming up behind," hissed Mrs P. "Off your windward tail feathers."

Mrs P carefully began to crawl backwards on Soren. He adjusted his wings. For even with her light weight, as she moved he could feel his balance shift. Mrs P could smell the crow's stinky breath as it closed in. Soren began to dive. Mrs P continued to make her way towards the stiffer and coarser tail feathers. A great whiff of crow stench engulfed her. Mrs Plithiver raised her head in the direction of the foul odour and began screaming, "Scum of the sky, curse of the earth, riffraff of the Yonder. Scurrilous crowilous," she ranted.

The Yonder was what all blind snakes called the sky because it was so far away, about as far away as anything could be for a snake. But Mrs P saved her most poisonous insult for last – "Wet pooper!" Blind snakes were especially impressed by owls' digestive systems, which allowed them to compress certain parts of waste into neat pellets that they yarped up through their mouths, as opposed to other disgusting birds whom they referred to as 'wet poopers'. The crow seemed to brake mid-flight. His beak fell open, his wings folded.

Crows are simple birds. And what this crow had just seen and heard – a snake hissing curses and rising from the back feathers of an owl – stunned him. He went 'yeep', which meant that he simply froze in flight and began to plummet to earth.

The crows by this time had begun to disappear. Twilight flew up to Soren's windward side. "Digger's hurt," he said.

Indeed, when Soren looked in the direction of Digger, he saw the Burrowing Owl tipping dangerously to one side. "We've got to find a place to land."

Gylfie flew up breathlessly. "I don't know how much longer Digger can last. He's not flying straight at all."

"Which way is he tipping?" Mrs P asked.

"Downwind," said Twilight.

"Quick!" she ordered. "Let's get over there. I might be able to help."

"You?" Twilight asked somewhat incredulously.

"Remember, dear, how Digger had been asking me to ride on his back in the desert? This might just be the time."

A few seconds later they were coming in on Digger's upwind wing.

"Digger," Soren said, "we know you're hurt."

"I don't know if I can make it," the Burrowing Owl groaned. "Oh, if I could only walk."

"There's a stand of trees really close," Soren said. "Mrs P has an idea that might help you."

"What's that?"

"She's going to get on your good wing. That will tip your injured wing up again, lighten the drag on it. Gylfie meanwhile will fly under your bad wing and create a little updraft for it. It might work."

"I don't know," Digger moaned miserably.

"Faith, boy! Faith!" exhorted Mrs Plithiver. "Now let's get on with it."

"I really don't think I can make it," Digger gasped.

"You can, boy! You can!" said Mrs P. Her voice grew amazingly strong. "You shall go on to the finish. You shall fly to the forests, to the trees, to Hoolemere. You have defended yourself against these crows. You have strode across deserts. You shall defend yourself now by flying. You shall fly into the wind, into the light, into this new day. Whatever the cost, you shall fly on. You shall not fail or falter. You shall not weaken. You shall finish the flight." Mrs P's voice swelled in the growing light of the morning and somehow it filled them all with new courage.

Now Soren flew in so close to Digger that his wing was touching the tip of Digger's good wing. They were ready for the transfer. "Now, Mrs P! Go!"

The old nest snake began to slither out on to Soren's wing. Soren felt the pressure of air around his body and the cushions of wind under his wings shift. The air surrounding him seemed to fray. He had to concentrate hard not to go into a roll. But if he was frightened, he could not imagine what Mrs P was feeling as she blindly slithered out to the tip of his wing and began the precarious transfer to Digger.

"Almost there, dear, almost there. Steady now. Steady."

Suddenly, she was gone. His wing felt light. Soren turned his head. She had made it. She was now crawling up towards the base of Digger's wing. It was working. Digger's flight grew even.

"We're bringin' him in! We're bringin' him in!" Twilight shouted triumphantly. Creating direct updrafts that supported Digger's flight, Twilight flew below, along with Gylfie who, under the injured wing, was doing the same.

Finally, they landed in a large spruce tree. There was a perfect hollow for them to spend the day in, and Mrs Plithiver immediately launched into a frenzy of action. "I need worms! Big fat ones, and leeches. Quick – all of you! Go out and get me what I need. I'll stay here with Digger."

Mrs Plithiver crawled on to Digger's back. "Now, this won't hurt, dear, but I just want to feel what those awful crows did to you." Gently, she began flicking her forked tongue over his wound. "It's not deep. The best thing I can do is to curl up right on the wound until they come back. A snake's skin can be very healing in many cases. We're a little too dry for the long run, however. That's why I want the worms."

Soon the owls were back with the worms and leeches that Mrs P had ordered. She directed Soren to place two leeches on the wound. "That will cleanse it. I can't tell you how filthy crows are!"

After the leeches had done their work, Mrs Plithiver pulled them off and gently replaced them with two fat worms.

Digger sighed. "That feels so good."

"Yes, there's nothing like a fat slimy worm for relief of a wound. You'll be fit to fly by tomorrow night."

"Thank you, Mrs P. Thank you so much." Digger blinked at Mrs P, and there was a look in his large yellow eyes of disbelief that he could have ever considered such a snake a meal – which, as a desert owl, Digger often did.

Within the spruce tree where they perched, there was another hollow that housed a family of Masked Owls.

"They look almost exactly like you, Soren," Gylfie said. "And they're coming to visit."

"Masked Owls look nothing like me," Soren replied. Everyone was always saying this. He had heard his parents complain about it. Yes, they had white faces and buff-coloured wings, but they had many more spots on their breasts and head.

"They're coming here to visit?" Mrs P said. "Oh dear, the place is a mess. We can't receive company now. I'm nursing this poor owl."

"They heard about the mobbing," Gylfie said. "We're even a little bit famous."

"Why's that?" asked Soren.

"I guess that gang of crows is really bad. They couldn't believe we battled back and survived," Gylfie replied.

Soon, they heard the Masked Owls arriving. One poked her head in. "Mind if we visit?" It was the female owl. And although Masked Owls belonged to the same species of owls as Soren's family, which were Barn Owls, and they were all known as Tytos, they were hardly identical.

"See what I mean?" Soren whispered to Gylfie. "They are completely different. Look at how much bigger and darker they are." The point was lost on Gylfie.

"We wanted to meet the brave owls who battled the crows," said the owl's mate.

"Yeah, how'd you ever do that?" a very young owlet who had barely fledged peeped up.

"Oh, it wasn't all that hard," Twilight said and dipped his head almost modestly.

"Not that hard!" Mrs Plithiver piped up. "Hardest thing I've ever done!"

"You!" the male Masked Owl exclaimed.

"She certainly had nothing to do with the defeat of the crows. She's a nest-maid," his mate said in a haughty voice.

Mrs Plithiver seemed to fade a bit. She nudged one of the worms that had begun to crawl off Digger's wing.

"She had everything to do with it!" Soren bristled up and suddenly seemed almost as big as the Masked Owls. "If it hadn't been for Mrs P, I would have been dive-bombed from the rear and poor Digger would have never made it back."

The Masked Owls blinked. "Well, well." The large female chuffed and stepped nervously from one talon to another. "We just aren't used to such aggressive behaviour from our nest-maids. Ours are rather meek, I guess, compared to this... what do you call her?"

"Her name is Mrs Plithiver," Soren said slowly and distinctly, with the contempt in his voice poorly concealed.

"Yes, yes," the female replied nervously. "Well, we discourage our nest-maids from socially mingling with us at any time, really."

"That was hardly a party, what happened up there in the sky, ma'am," Twilight said hotly.

"Well, now tell me, young'uns," said the male as if he was desperately trying to change the subject. "Where are you heading? What are your plans?"

"We're going to Hoolemere and the Great Ga'Hoole Tree," Soren said.

"Oh, how interesting," the female replied in a voice that had a sneer embedded in it.

"Oh, Mummy," said the young owlet. "That's the place I was telling you about. Can't we go?"

"Nonsense. You know how we feel about make-believe."

The little owlet dipped his head in embarrassment.

"It's not make-believe," said Gylfie.

"Oh, you can't be serious, young'un," said the male. "It's just a story, an old legend."

"Let me tell you something," said the female, whom Soren disliked more and more by the second. "It does not do any good to believe in things you cannot see, touch or feel. It is a waste of time. From the look of your flight feathers' development, not to mention your talons, it is apparent that you are either fly-aways or orphans. Why else would you be out cavorting about the skies at such dangerous hours of the morning? I think your parents would be ashamed of you. I can tell you have good breeding." She looked directly at Soren and blinked.

Soren thought he might explode with anger. How did this owl know what his parents might think? How dare she suggest that she knew them so well that she knew they would be ashamed of him?

And then there was a small soft, hissing voice. "I am ashamed of anyone who has eyes and still cannot see." It was Mrs Plithiver. She slithered from the corner in the hollow. "But, of course, to see with two eyes is a very common thing."

"What is she talking about?" said the male.

"What happened to the old days when servants served and were quiet? Imagine a nest-maid going on like this," said the female.

"Oh, yes," said Mrs Plithiver. "And I shall go on a bit more, if you permit me." She proceeded to arrange herself in a lovely coil and swung her head towards Soren.

"Of course, Mrs Plithiver. Please go on," Soren said.

"I am a blind snake, but who says I cannot see as much as you?" And then she swung her head sharply towards the female Masked Owl, who seemed startled, and it did appear indeed as if Mrs Plithiver was looking directly at her with her two small eye dents. "Who says I cannot see? To see with eyes is so ordinary. I see with my whole body – my skin, my bones, the coiling of my spine. And between the slow beats of my very slow heart, I sense the world here and beyond. I know the Yonder. Oh, yes. I have known it even before I ever flew in it. But before that day did I say it did not exist? What a fool you would have called me, milady, had I said your sky does not exist because I cannot see it nor can I fly. And what a fool you are to believe that Hoolemere does not exist."

"Well, I never!" gasped the Masked Owl. She looked at her mate in astonishment. "She called me a fool!"

But Mrs Plithiver continued. "Sky does not exist merely in the wings of birds, an impulse in their feathers and blood and bone. Sky becomes the Yonder for all creatures if they free their hearts and their brains to feel, to know in the deepest ways. And when the Yonder calls, it speaks to all of us, be it sky, be it Hoolemere, be it heaven or glaumora." Glaumora was the special heaven where the souls of owls went. "So perhaps," Mrs Plithiver continued, "there are some who need to lose their eyes to discover their sight." Mrs P nodded her head gracefully and slithered back into the corner. A stunned silence fell upon the hollow.

The four young owls waited until First Black to leave. "No more flying during light," Mrs Plithiver said as she coiled into Soren's neck feathers. "Agreed?"

"Agreed," the owls replied at once.

They were now skirting the edges of the Kingdom of Tyto, the kingdom from which Soren's family came. Although he was as alert as ever and flying most skilfully, Mrs Plithiver could sense a quietness in him. He did not join in the others' flight chatter. She knew he must have been thinking of his parents, his lost family and, in particular, his sister, Eglantine, whom he loved most dearly. The chances of finding any of them were almost zero and she knew that Soren knew this, but still she could feel his pain. Yet he had not exactly described it as pain. He had once said to Mrs P shortly after they had been reunited that he had felt as if there were a hole in his gizzard, and that when he and Mrs P had found each other again, it was as if a little bit of the hole had been mended. But Mrs P knew that despite the patch she had provided there was still a hole.

When the first stars began to fade, they looked for a place to land and settle in before morning. It was Gylfie who spotted an old sycamore, silvery in this moonless night. The full moon had begun its dwenking many nights before, growing slimmer and slimmer until it dwenked and disappeared entirely, and there would not be a trace of it for another night or so until the newing began.

CHAPTER TWO

In the Company of Sooty Owls

"Oh yes, dear. I've heard of it, but you know they say it's just a story, a legend."

"Well, it's not exactly that, Sweetums," said the Sooty Owl's mate.

The four owls had been warmly welcomed into the large and spacious hollow in the sycamore by a family of Sooty Owls. These two owls were much nicer than the Masked Owls. Indeed very, very nice and, Soren thought, very, very boring. They called each other by nicknames – Sweetums and Swatums. They never said a cross word. Everything was just perfect. The children had all grown up.

"Left the nest a year ago. Still nearby," said Swatums, the male. "But who knows, Sweetums might come up with another clutch of eggs in the new breeding season. And if she doesn't, well, we two are enough company for each other." Then they began preening each other.

It seemed to Soren and Gylfie that they preened incessantly. They always had their beaks in each other's feathers, except, of course, when they were hunting. And when they were hunting they were exceptional killers. It was as predators that these Sooty Owls became the most interesting. Sweetums and Swatums were simply deadly, and Soren had to admit he had never eaten so well. Twilight had told them to watch carefully, for Sooty Owls were among the rare owls that went after tree prey and not just ground prey.

So tonight they were all feasting on three of a type of possum that they called sugar gliders. They were the sweetest things that any of the young band of owls had ever tasted. Maybe that was why the two Sooties called each other Sweetums and Swatums. They had simply eaten too many sweet things. Perhaps eating a steady diet of sugar gliders made an owl ooze with gooiness. Soren thought he was going to go stark raving yoicks if he had to listen to their gooey talk a moment longer, but luckily they were now, in their own boring way, discussing the Great Ga'Hoole Tree.

Sweetums was questioning her mate. "Well, what do you mean, Swatums, by 'not exactly'? Isn't it either a legend or not? I mean, it's not really real."

"Well, Sweetums, some say it's simply invisible."

"What's simple about being invisible?" Gylfie asked.

"Ohh, hooo-hooo." The two Sooty Owls were convulsed with laughter. "Doesn't she remind you of Tibby, Swatums?" Then there was more cooing and giggling and disgusting preening. Soren felt that Gylfie's question was a perfectly sensible one. What, indeed, was simple about invisibleness?

"Well, young'uns," Swatums answered, "there is nothing simple. It's just that it has been said that the Great Ga'Hoole Tree is invisible. That it grows on the island in the middle of a vast sea, a sea called Hoolemere that is nearly as wide as an ocean. A sea that is always wrapped in fog, an island feathered in blizzards and a tree veiled in mist."

"So," said Twilight, "it's not really invisible, it's just bad weather."

"Not exactly," replied Swatums. Twilight cocked his head. "It seems that for some the fog lifts, the blizzards stop and the mist blows away."

"For some?" asked Gylfie.

"For those who believe." Swatums paused and then sniffed in disdain. "But do they say what? Believe in what? No. You see, that is the problem. Owls with fancy ideas – ridiculous! That's how you get into trouble. Sweetums and I don't believe in fancy ideas. Fancy ideas don't keep the belly full and the gizzard grinding. Sugar gliders, plump rats, voles – that's what counts." Sweetums nodded and Swatums went over and began preening her for the millionth time that day.

Soren knew in that moment that even if he were starving to death, he would still find Sweetums and Swatums the most boring owls on Earth.

That late afternoon as they nestled in the hollow, waiting for First Black, Gylfie stirred sleepily. "You awake, Soren?"

"Yeah. I can't wait to get to Hoolemere."

"Me neither. But I was wondering," Gylfie said.

"Wondering what?"

"Do you think that Streak and Zan love each other as much as Sweetums and Swatums?" Streak and Zan were two Bald Eagles who had helped them in the desert when Digger had been attacked by the lieutenants from St Aggie's – the very ones who had earlier eaten Digger's brother, Flick. The two eagles had seemed deeply devoted to each other. Yet Zan could not utter a sound. Her tongue had been torn out in battle.

What an interesting question, Soren thought. His own parents never preened each other as constantly as Sweetums and Swatums, and they hadn't called each other gooey names, but he had never doubted their love for each other. "I don't know," he replied. "It's hard thinking about mates. I mean, can you imagine ever having a mate or what he might be like?"

There was a long pause. "Honestly, no," replied Gylfie.

They heard Twilight stir in his sleep.

"If I never taste another sugar glider it will be too soon." Digger belched softly. "They keep repeating on me."

The four owls had left at First Black and bid their farewells to the Sooties. They had now alighted on a tree limb with a good view down the valley. They were looking for a creek – any creek that could feed into a river that hopefully would be the River Hoole, which they could follow to the Sea of Hoolemere.

"What do you mean 'keep repeating on you'?" Soren asked, imagining little possums gliding in and out of Digger's beak.

"Just an expression. My dad used to say that after

he ate centipedes." Digger sighed. "And then Ma would say, 'Well, of course they keep repeating on you, dear. You eat something that has all those legs, they're probably still running around inside you'."

Gylfie, Twilight and Soren burst out laughing.

Digger sighed again. "My mum was really funny. I miss her jokes."

"Come on," said Gylfie. "You'll be OK."

"But everything is so different here. I don't live in trees. Never have in my life. I'm a Burrowing Owl. I lived in desert burrows. I don't hunt these silly creatures that glide and fly about through the limbs. I miss the taste of snake and crawly things that pick up the dirt. Whoops, sorry, Mrs P."

"Don't apologise, Digger. Most owls do eat snakes – not usually blind snakes, since we tend their nests – but other snakes. Soren's parents were particularly sensitive and, out of respect for me, would not eat any snake."

Twilight had hopped to a higher limb to see if he could see any trace of a creek that might lead to a river.

"He's not going to be able to see anything in this light. I don't care how good his eyes are. A black trickle of a creek in a dark forest – forget it," Gylfie said.

Suddenly, Soren cocked his head, first one way, then the other.

"What is it, Soren?" Digger asked.

"You hear something?" Twilight flew down and landed on a thin branch that creaked under his weight.

"Hush!" Soren said.

They all fell silent and watched as the Barn Owl tipped, cocked and pivoted his head in a series of small movements. And, finally, Soren heard something. "There is a trickle. I hear it. It's not a lot of water, but I can hear that it begins in reeds and then it starts to slide over stones."

Barn Owls were known for their extremely sensitive hearing. They could contract and expand the muscles of their facial disks to funnel the sound source to their unevenly placed earholes. The other owls were in awe of their friend's abilities.

"Let's go. I'll lead," Soren said.

It was one of the few times anyone except Twilight had flown in the point position.

As Soren flew, he kept angling his head so that his two ears, one lower and one higher, could precisely locate the source of the water. Within a few minutes, they had found a trickle and that trickle turned into a stream, a stream full of the music of gently tumbling water. Then by dawn that stream had become a river – the River Hoole.

"A masterful job of triangulation," Gylfie cried. "Simply masterful, Soren. You are a premier navigator."

"What's she saying?" Digger asked.

"She's saying that Soren got us here. Big words, little owl." But it was evident that Twilight was impressed.

"So now what do we do?" Digger asked.

"Follow the river to the Sea of Hoolemere," Twilight said. "Come on. We still have a few hours until First Light."

"More flying?" Digger asked.

"What? You want to walk?" Twilight replied.

"I wouldn't mind. My wings are tired. And it's not just my wound. It's healed."

The three other owls stared at Digger in dismay. Gylfie hopped out on the tree branch they had landed on and peered intently at Digger. "Wings don't get tired. That's impossible."

"Well, mine do. Can't we rest up a bit?" Burrowing Owls, like Digger, were in fact known for their running abilities. Blessed with long, featherless legs, they could stride across the deserts as well as fly over them. But their flight skills were not as strong as those of other owls.

"I'm hungry, anyway," said Soren. "Let me see if I can catch us something."

"Please, no sugar gliders," Digger added.

CHAPTER THREE

Twilight Shows Off

They had settled into the hollow of a fir tree and were eating some voles that Soren had brought back from his hunting expedition.

"Refreshing, isn't it, after sugar gliders?" Gylfie said.

"Hmmm!" Digger smacked his beak and made a satisfied sound.

"What do you think the Great Ga'Hoole Tree will be like?" Soren said dreamily, as a little bit of vole tail hung from his beak.

"Different from St Aggie's, that's for sure," Gylfie offered.

"Do you think they know about St Aggie's – the raids, the egg snatching, the... the..." Soren hesitated.

"The cannibalism," Digger said. "You might as well say it, Soren. Don't try to protect me. I've seen the worst and I know it."

They had all seen the worst.

Twilight, who was huge to start with, was beginning to swell up in fury. Soren knew what was coming. Twilight was not thinking about the owls of Ga'Hoole, those noble guardian knights of the sky. He was thinking about those ignoble, contemptible, basest of the base, monstrous owls of St Aggie's. Twilight had been orphaned so young that he had not the slightest scrap of memory of his parents. For a long time, he had led a kind of vagabond, orphan life. Indeed, Twilight had lived with all sorts of odd animals, even a fox at one point, which was why he never hunted fox.

Like all Great Greys, he was considered a powerful and ruthless predator, but Twilight prided himself on being, as he called it, an owl from the Orphan School of Tough Learning. He was completely self-taught. He had lived in burrows with foxes, flown with eagles. He was strong and a real fighter. And there was not a modest hollow bone in Twilight's body. He was powerful, a brilliant flier, and he was fast. As fast with his talons as with his beak. In a minute they all knew that the air would become shrill as he sang his own praises and jabbed and stabbed at an imaginary foe. Twilight's shadow began to flicker in the dim light of the hollow as his voice, deep and thrumming, started to chant.

We're going to bash them birds,
Them rat-feathered birds.
Them bad-butt owls ain't never heard
'Bout Gylfie, Soren, Dig and Twilight.
Just let them get to feel my bite
Their li'l ol' gizzards gonna turn to pus
And our feathers hardly mussed.
Oh me. Oh my. They gonna cry.
One look at Twilight,
They know they're gonna die.
I see fear in their eyes
And that ain't all.
They know that Twilight's got the gall.
Gizzard with gall that makes him great
And every bad owl gonna turn to bait.

Jab, jab – then a swipe and hook with the right talon. Twilight danced around the hollow. The air churned with his shadow fight, and Gylfie, the tiniest of them all, had to hang on tight. It was like a small hurricane in the hollow. Then, finally, his movements slowed and he pranced off into a corner.

"Got that out of your system, Twilight?" Gylfie asked.

"What do you mean 'out of my system'?"

"Your aggression."

Twilight made a slightly contemptuous sound that came from the back of his throat. "Big words, little owl." This was something Twilight often said to Gylfie. Gylfie did have a tendency to use big words.

"Well now, young'uns," Mrs P was speaking up. "Let's not get into it. I think, Gylfie, that in the face of cannibalism, aggression or going stark raving yoicks and absolutely annihilating the cannibals is perfectly appropriate."

"More big words but I like them. I like them, Mrs P," Twilight hooted his delight.

Soren, however, remained quiet. He was thinking. He was still wondering what the Great Ga'Hoole Tree would be like. What would those noble owls think of an owl like Twilight – so unrefined, yet powerful. So cheeky, but loyal – so angry, but true?

CHAPTER FOUR

Get Out! Get Out!

They had left the hollow of the fir tree at First Black. The night was racing with ragged clouds. The forest covering was thick beneath them so they flew low to keep the River Hoole in sight, which sometimes narrowed and only appeared as the smallest glimmer of a thread of water. The trees thinned and Twilight said that he thought the region below was known as The Beaks. For a while, they seemed to lose the strand of the river, and there appeared to be many other small threadlike creeks or tributaries. They were, of course, worried they might have lost the Hoole, but if they had their doubts they dared not even think about them for a sliver of a second. For doubts, each one feared in the deepest parts of their quivering gizzards, might be like an owl sickness – like greyscale or beak rot – contagious and able to spread from owl to owl.

How many false creeks, streams and even rivers had they followed so far, only to be disappointed? But now Digger called out, "I see something!" All of their gizzards quickened. "It's, it's... whitish... well, greyish."

"Ish? What in Glaux's name is 'ish'?" Twilight hooted.

"It means," Gylfie said in her clear voice, "that it's not exactly white, and it's not exactly grey."

"I'll have a look. Hold your flight pattern until I get back."

The huge Great Grey Owl began a power dive. He was not gone long before he returned. "And you know why it's not exactly grey and not exactly white?" Twilight did not wait for an answer. "Because it's smoke."

"Smoke?" The other three seemed dumbfounded.

"You do know what smoke is?" Twilight asked. He tried to remember to be patient with these owls who had seen and experienced so much less than he had.

"Sort of," Soren replied. "You mean there's a forest fire down there? I've heard of those."

"Oh, no. Nothing that big. Maybe once it was. But, really, the forests of The Beaks are minor ones. Second-rate. Few and far between and not much to catch fire."

"Spontaneous combustion – no doubt," Gylfie said. Twilight gave the little Elf Owl a withering look. Always trying to steal his show with the big words. He had no idea what spontaneous combustion was and he doubted if Gylfie did, either. But he let it go for the moment. "Come on, let's go explore."

They alighted on the forest floor at the edge of where the smoke was the thickest. It seemed to be coming out of a cave beneath a stone outcropping. There was a scattering of a few glowing coals on the ground and charred pieces of wood. "Digger," Twilight said, "can you dig as well as you can walk with those naked legs of yours?"

"You bet. How do you think we fix up our burrows or make them bigger? We don't just settle for what we happen upon."

"Well, start digging and show the rest of us how. We've got to bury these coals before a wind comes up and carries them off and really gets a fire going."

It was hard work burying the coals, especially for Gylfie, who was the tiniest and had the shortest legs of all. "I wonder what happened here?" Gylfie said as she paused to look around. Her eyes settled on what she thought was a charred piece of wood, but something glinted through the blackness of the moonless night.

Glinted and curved into a familiar shape. Gylfie blinked. Her gizzard gave a little twitch and as if in a trance she walked over towards the object.

"Battle claws!" she gasped. From inside the cave came a terrible moan. "Get out! Get out!"

But they couldn't get out! They couldn't move. Between them and the mouth of the cave, gleaming eyes, redder than any of the live coals, glowered and there was a horrible rank smell. Two curved white fangs sliced the darkness.

"Bobcat!" Twilight roared.

The four owls simultaneously lifted their eight wings in powerful upstrokes. The bobcat shrieked below, a terrible sky-shattering shriek. Soren had never heard anything like it. It had all happened so suddenly that Soren had even forgotten to drop the coal that he had in his beak.

"Good Glaux, Soren!" Gylfie said as she saw her dear friend's face bathed in the red light of the radiant coal.

Soren dropped it immediately.

There was another shriek. A shadow blacker than the night seemed to leap into the air, then plummet to the ground, writhing and yowling in pain.

"Well, bust my gizzard!" Twilight shouted. "Soren, you dropped that coal right on the cat! What a shot!"

"I – what?"

"Come on, we're going in for him – for the kill."

"The kill?" Soren said blankly.

"Follow me. Aim for his eyes. Gylfie, stay clear of his tail. I'll go for the throat. Digger, take a flank."

The four owls flew down in a deadly wedge. Soren aimed for the eyes, but one was already useless, as the coal had done its work and a still-sizzling socket wept small embers. Digger sunk his talons into an exposed flank as the bobcat writhed on the ground, and Gylfie stuck one of her talons down the largest nostril that Soren had ever seen. Twilight made a quick slice at the throat and blood spattered the night. The cat was no longer howling. It lay in a heap on the forest floor, its face smouldering from the coal. The smell of singed fur filled the night as the bobcat's pulse grew weaker and the blood poured out from the deep gash in its throat.

"Was he after the battle claws – a bobcat?" Soren turned to Gylfie.

When the two owls had been at St Aggie's, Grimble, the old Boreal Owl who had died helping them escape, had told them how the warriors of St Aggie's could not make their own battle claws so they scavenged them from battlefields. But a bobcat? Why would a bobcat need battle claws? They stared at the long sharp claws that extended from the paws of the cat and looked deadlier than any battle claws.

"No," Twilight said quietly. He had flown over to the cave and now stood in its opening. "The cat was after what was in here."

"What's that?" the three other owls asked at once.

"A dying owl," Mrs Plithiver said as she slithered out from the cave where she had taken refuge. "Come in. I think he wants to speak, if he has any more breath in him."

The owls moved into the cave opening. There was a mass of brown feathers collapsed by a shallow pit that still glowed with embers. It was a Barred Owl. Although that was hard to tell, for the white bars of his plumage were bloodstained and his beak seemed to jut out at a peculiar angle. "Don't blame the cat," the Barred Owl moaned. "Only here after... after... they—"

"After they what, sir?" Gylfie stepped closer to the skewed beak and bent her head to better hear the weak voice.

"They wanted the battle claws, didn't they?" Soren bobbed his head down towards the dying owl. Did he move his head slightly as if to nod? But the Barred Owl's breath was going, was growing shallower.

"Was it St Aggie's?" Glyfie spoke softly.

"I wish it had been St Aggie's. It was something far worse. Believe me – if St Aggie's – Oh! You only wish!" The owl sighed and was dead.

The four owls blinked at one another and were silent for several moments. "You only wish!" Digger repeated. "Does he mean there's something worse than St Aggie's?"

"How could there be?" Soren said.

"What is this place?" Gylfie said. "Why are there battle claws here but it isn't a battlefield? If it had been, we would have seen other owls, wounded or dead."

They turned towards the Great Grey. "Twilight?" Soren asked.

But for once, Twilight seemed stumped. "I'm not sure. I've heard tell of owls – very clever owls that live apart, never mate, not really belonging to any kingdom. Do for themselves for the most part. Sometimes hire out for battles. Hireclaws, I think they call them. Maybe this was one. And The Beaks is a funny place, you know. Not many forests. Mostly ridges like the ones we've been flying over the last day or so. A few woods in between. So not a lot of places for owls to end up. No really big trees with big hollows. Probably a real loner, this fellow."

They looked down at the dead Barred Owl.

"What should we do with him?" Soren asked. "I hate to leave him here for the next bobcat to come along. He tried to warn us, after all. He said, 'Get out! Get out!'"

It was Digger who spoke next in a quavery voice. "And, you know, I don't think he was warning us about the bobcat."

"You think," Gylfie said in a quiet steady voice, "that it was about these others, the ones worse than St Aggie's?"

Digger nodded.

"But we can't just leave him. This was a brave owl... a noble owl." Soren spoke vehemently, "He was noble even if he didn't live at the Great Tree as a knightly owl."

Twilight stepped forwards. "Soren's right. He was a brave owl. I don't want to leave him for dirty old scavengers. If it's not the bobcats, it'll be the crows; if not crows, vultures."

"But what can we do with him?" Digger said.

"I've heard of burial hollows, high up in trees," Twilight said. "When I was with a Whiskered Screech family in Ambala that's what they did when their grandmother died."

"It's going to take too long to find a hollow in The Beaks," Gylfie now spoke. "You said it yourself,

Twilight – it's a second-rate forest, no big trees."

Soren was looking around. "This owl lived in this cave. Look, you can tell. There's some fresh pellets just outside, and there's a stash of nuts and over there, a vole killed not long ago – probably his next dinner... I think we should—"

"We can't leave him in the cave," Gylfie interrupted. "Even if it is his home. Another bobcat could come along and find him."

"But Soren is right," Digger said. "His spirit is here." Digger was a very odd owl. Whereas most owls were consumed with the practical world of hunting, flying and nesting, Digger – with his legs better for running than his wings were for flying, with his inclination for burrows rather than hollows – was undeniably an impractical owl. But perhaps because he was not focused on the commonplace, the ordinary drudgeries and small joys of owl life, his mind was freer to range. And range it did into the sphere of the spiritual, of the meaning of life, of the possibilities of an afterlife. And it was the afterlife of the brave Barred Owl that seemed to concern him now. "His spirit is in this cave. I feel it."

"So what do we do?" Twilight asked.

Soren looked around slowly at the cave. His dark eyes, like polished stones, studied the walls. "He had many fires in this cave. Look at the walls – as sooty as a Sooty Owl's wings. I think he made things with fires in this pit right here. I think..." Soren spoke very slowly. "I think we should burn him."

"Burn him?" the other three owls repeated quietly.

"Yes. Right here in this pit. The embers are still burning. It will be enough." The owls nodded to one another in silent agreement. It seemed right.

So the four owls, as gently as they could, rolled the dead Barred Owl on to the coals with their talons.

"Do we have to stay and watch?" Gylfie asked as the first feathers began to ignite.

"No!" Soren said, and they all followed him out of the cave entrance and flew into the night.

They rose on a series of updrafts and then circled the clearing where the cave had been. Three times they circled as they watched the smoke curl out from the mouth of the cave. Mrs Plithiver moved forwards through the thick feathers of Soren's shoulders and leaned out towards one of his ears. "I am proud of you, Soren. You have protected a brave owl against the indignities of scavengers." Soren wasn't sure what the word 'indignities' meant, but he hoped what they had done was right for an owl he believed to be

CHAPTER FIVE

The Mirror Lakes

Mrs Plithiver was worried. Yes, it was understandable that the owls had been unnerved by the Barred Owl's ominous words. The very notion of something worse than St Aggie's was indeed a horrifying thought. They needed some time to rest, to unwind. Twilight said that he had heard about this place that was so lovely, endless plump voles scampering about, no crows at all, tree hollows in which moss as soft as down grew. Why, it sounded irresistible. And it was! And now Mrs Plithiver was nearly frantic in this resplendent place. It was perfectly clear to her that the owls would be content to stay here forever.

But life was too easy in this region on the edge of

The Beaks, which was called the Mirror Lakes. She knew it wasn't good for them and beneath the gleaming surfaces of the lakes, within the quiet verdant beauty of this crowless place, she sensed something dangerous. She could have just swatted Twilight and his big mouth. The four owls seemed to have forgotten their ordeal in the forest with the bobcat and the dying Barred Owl entirely. Shortly after they had turned to fly in the direction of the Mirror Lakes, they began to encounter the wonderful rolling drafts of air that curled up from the rippled landscape below and provided them with matchless flying. The sensation was sublime as they gently floated over the sculpted air currents without having to waggle a wing. The rhythm was mesmerising and then, shortly before dawn, sparkling below between the ripples of the land, were several still lakes, so clear, so glistening that they reflected every single star and cloud in the sky.

The Mirror Lakes were like an oasis in the otherwise barren landscape of The Beaks. The owls had chosen trees near the lake that had perfect-sized hollows, all cushioned with the loveliest of mosses.

"It's simply dreamy here," Gylfie said for perhaps the hundredth time. And that, precisely, was the problem. It was dreamy. Not just dreamy – but a dream. It didn't seem real with its plentiful game so easy to hunt, and the rolling drafts of warm air so tempting that, against Mrs P's orders, the owls had begun to take playful flights in broad daylight. But perhaps worst of all were the tranquil gleaming lakes themselves. These owls had never been around such clear water. There was no silt, no mud, no muck and bits swirling about in it. So they could see their reflections perfectly. Not one of these owls, except for Twilight, had ever seen its reflection. And even Twilight had never seen his so clearly.

It had all started with Soren, actually, when Gylfie pointed out to him that he had a smudge on his beak from the coal that he had picked up and dropped on the bobcat. Soren had flown a short distance from the tree where they had found a hollow, to the edge of the lake, to clean up. Until that time, Soren had thought that water was only for drinking and occasionally – very occasionally – for washing. But when he peered into the lake he nearly fainted.

"Da!" he gasped.

"It's not your da. It's you, dear," Mrs Plithiver said. For although she was blind, Mrs P knew about reflections in much the same way she knew so many other things that she could not see. "You've probably never seen your face fully fledged."

"It's all white, just like Da's. I'm so, so—"

"Handsome?" Mrs Plithiver said.

"Well, yeah." Soren muffled a nervous churr, slightly embarrassed to admit it.

Slightly, but no more! That was, indeed, the end of Soren's embarrassment as well as his modesty, and the end of the other owls' as well. They were all soon nodding over the mirror of the lake, admiring themselves. And when they weren't gazing at their reflections from the edge, they were flying above the lakes, marvelling at their fabulous flight manoeuvres and pitching 'wingies', as they called it when they rolled off rising drafts of air. Twilight was, of course, the worst of all because he was so boastful to begin with. Mrs Plithiver could hear him out there now, hooting about his beauty, his muscular physique, the fluffiness of his feathers, while he tumbled over and under a roll of air.

"Look at me bounce off this cloud!" And then for the tenth time that day, Twilight sang his "I Am More Beautiful Than a Cloud" song.

What is as fleecy as a cloud,
As majestic and shimmering as the breaking dawn,
As gorgeous as the sun is strong?
Why, it's ME!

Twilight, the Great Grey,
Tiger of the sky –
Light of the Night,
Most beautiful,
An avian delight.
I beam –
I gleam –
I'm a livin' flying dream.
Watch me roll off this cloud and pop on back.
This is flying,
I ain't no hack.

"But," Mrs Plithiver said with a hiss that sizzled, "you *ain't*, as you say, 'rolling off clouds'!" Because, as Mrs Plithiver could sense, the clouds were too high that day, and Twilight was flying too low to reach them as he admired himself in the Mirror Lakes. In actuality, Twilight was flying off the reflections of clouds that quivered on the glasslike surface of the lake. And that, Mrs Plithiver concluded, was the heart of the problem with all the owls. They were mistaking the world of image and reflection for the real world. The Mirror Lakes had transfixed them. And in their transfixed state they had forgotten all they had fought for and fought against. Had they once spoken of the Great

Ga'Hoole Tree or its noble owls since they had arrived at this cursed place? Had they ever mentioned St Aggie's and its terrors? Had Soren even once thought of his dear family except the first time he caught his reflection in the lake? And what about Eglantine? Did he ever think of her and what might have happened to his poor sister?

This was a very strange place. It was not just the Mirror Lakes and the thick soft moss and the perfect tree hollows and the plentiful game. Suddenly, Mrs Plithiver realised that in the rest of the kingdoms they had flown through it was becoming early winter, but here it was still summer, full summer. She could smell it. The leaves were still green, the grasses supple, the earth warm. But it was poisonous! They had to get out of here. This place was as dangerous as St Aggie's.

"Come here this instant! All of you!" It was the closest a hissing snake ever got to a snarl.

Soren jerked his head up from admiring his beak in the surface of the pond. He rather liked the smudge on it. He thought it added 'character' to his face, as Gylfie said.

"Mrs P, what in Glaux's name?"

"I'll Glaux you!" she hissed.

Soren nearly fainted. He never had heard Mrs P swear, and at him, no less. It was like venom curling out into the air. The other owls alighted next to Soren.

"Hey," Twilight said, "did you catch that curled wingie I just did?"

"Racdrops on your curled wingie."

Now a deep hush fell upon the owls. Had Mrs Plithiver lost her mind? Racdrops. She had actually said racdrops!

"What's wrong, Mrs P?" Soren asked in a trembling voice.

"What's wrong? Look at me. Stop looking at yourselves in the lake this instant. I'll tell you what's wrong. You are a disgrace to your families."

"I have no family if you'll recall, Mrs P." Twilight yawned.

"Worse then! You are a disgrace to your species. The Great Grey Owls."

This really took Twilight aback. "My species?"

"Yes, indeed. All of you are, for that matter. You have all grown fat, lazy and vain, the lot of you. Why... why..." Mrs Plithiver stammered.

Soren felt something really bad was coming.

"You're no better than a bunch of wet poopers!" With that, there was a raucous outburst from a branch overhanging where they stood at the lake's edge, on which a dozen or more seagulls had alighted. The harsh gull laughter ricocheted off the lake and the reflections of the owls on its surface quivered and then seemed to shatter.

"We're getting out of here NOW!" Mrs Plithiver said in a near roar for a snake.

"What about crows? It's not dark yet."

"Tough!" she spat.

"Are you going to sacrifice us to crows?" Gylfie said in a very small voice.

"You're sacrificing yourself right here on the shores of this lake." And something sharper than the fiercest gaze of eyes bore into Gylfie's gizzard. Indeed, all the owls felt their gizzards twist and lurch.

"Get ready to fly! And Twilight—"

"Yes, ma'am."

"I'll fly point with you."

"Yes, ma'am." The Great Grey stooped down so that Mrs Plithiver could slither on to his broad shoulders.

Of all the owls, Twilight had been the most transfixed by Mrs P's outburst. And if Twilight was to fly point, as he usually did, Mrs P felt she was going to have to be there to keep him on course. He was a 'special needs' case if there ever was one. What, indeed, had the world come to if an old blind nest-maid snake had to navigate for a Great Grey Owl? Some sky tiger!

But she had to navigate as Twilight began to circle the lake a second time and dip his downwind wing, no doubt for a better look at himself, and, yes, singing under his breath his next favourite tune –

Oh, wings of silver spread on high,
Fierce eyes of golden light,
Across the clouds of purple hue
In sheer majestic flight –
Oh, Twilight!
Oh, Twilight, most beautiful of owls,
Who sculpts the air
Beyond compare.
With feathers so sublime,
An owl for now –
An owl for then –
An owl for all of time.

Mrs Plithiver had coiled up and was waving her head as a signal to a gull she sensed overhead. Suddenly, there was a big white splat that landed on the silver wings sublime.

"What in Glaux's name?" Twilight said.

"They like you, Twilight. Blessed, I dare say!"

Twilight flew straight out across the lake and never looked back.

CHAPTER SIX

The Ice Narrows

It seemed as if winter had been waiting for them as soon as the Mirror Lakes dropped behind them. Blasts of frigid air, swirling with ice, sleet and often hail, smacked into them. The rolling ridges of The Beaks had become sharper and steeper, sending up confusing currents. Ice began to form on their own beaks and, in a few minutes, Soren saw Gylfie spin out of control. Luckily, Twilight accelerated and managed to help her.

"Fly in my wake, Gylfie," he shouted over the roar of the wind. And then he swivelled his head back to the others. "Her wings have started to ice. Ours will too – soon. It's too dangerous to continue. We have to look for a place to land."

Almost as soon as Twilight had spoken of iced wings, Soren felt his own suddenly grow heavy. He turned his head and nearly gasped when he saw his plummels, the silkiest of all his feathers, that fringed the outer edges of his primaries. They were stiff with frost and the wind was whistling through them. *Great Glaux, I'm flying like a gull!*

It was not long before they found a tree. The hollow was a rather miserable little one. They could barely cram into it, and it was crawling with vermin.

"This is appalling!" Mrs Plithiver said. "I've never seen such an infestation."

"Isn't there some moss someplace?" Twilight asked, remembering the extraordinarily soft, thick moss of the Mirror Lakes.

"Well, if someone wants to go out and look, they can," Mrs P said. "In the meantime, I'll try and eat as many of these maggotty little creatures as possible."

Soren peeked out the hollow. "The wind's picked up. You can't even see out there. Snow's so thick on the ground, I doubt if we could find any moss if we did look."

"We can always pulp some of the pine needles," Gylfie said. "First, you beak them hard enough, then let them slide down to your first stomach – the one before the gizzard. Hold it there for just a while, and then yarp it all back up. The pine needles come out all mushy and when they dry they're almost as soft as moss. Actually, technically speaking, it is not called yarping. It's burping when its wet and not a pellet."

"Who cares – as long as it's soft?" Twilight muttered.

"I suppose it's worth a try," Digger said. "The thought of going out there into that blizzard is not appealing in the least."

So the owls leaned out from the protection of the hollow only far enough to snatch a beakful of pine needles. They all began beaking, then swallowing the wads down to their first stomachs and then burping. All the while, Mrs Plithiver busied herself with sucking up maggots and pinch beetles, and one or two small worms known as feather raiders – all of which were most unhygienic to the health of owls.

"I don't think I could eat another pinch beetle if my life depended on it," Mrs P groaned after more than an hour.

There was a huge watery gurgle that rippled through the hollow.

"What was that?" Digger said.

"Yours truly, burping here," Twilight said and opened his beak and let go with another hollow-shaking burp.

"Oh, I've got to try that!" Digger said. In no time the four owls were having a burping contest. They were laughing and hooting and having a grand old time as the blizzard outside raged. They had figured out prizes as well. There was a prize, of course, for the loudest, but then one for the most watery sound, and one for the most disgusting, and one for the prettiest and most refined. Although everyone expected Gylfie to win with the prettiest, Soren did, and Gylfie won for the most disgusting.

"Absolutely vulgar," muttered Mrs P.

But soon they became bored with that and they began to wonder when the blizzard would let up. And although not one of them would admit it, secretly their thoughts turned to the Mirror Lakes and they grew quieter and quieter as they tried to remember their lazy beautiful days, flying in spectacular arcs over the lakes' gleaming surface. And the food, the food was so good!

"Oh, what I wouldn't give for a nice vole," Soren sighed.

"You know, young'un, I think the wind is lessening. I think maybe we should take off." Mrs Plithiver sensed the four owls' thoughts turning to the Mirror Lakes. She simply couldn't allow that. So even though she did not truly believe that the wind was lessening, it was essential to get them flying again.

"You call this less?" Digger hooted from his downwind position.

"A bit, and believe me, dear, sitting there burping pine needles isn't going to get you any closer to the Great Ga'Hoole Tree."

But what would? thought Soren. They could barely see ahead, behind was thick with swirling snow, below was dense fog that not even a treetop could poke through, and, off to windward, sheets of frigid air seemed to tumble from somewhere.

"There are cliffs to windward." Twilight drifted back from his point position. "I think that if we could get under the lee of them we might be protected and able to fly better."

"Sounds like it's worth a try. We'd better get Gylfie between us," Soren said.

The owls had become adept at creating a still place for Gylfie in the centre of their flying wedge formation when the winds became too tumultuous for the Elf Owl. Gylfie moved into that spot now. "All right, let's crab upwind," Twilight hooted over the fury of the blizzard.

Crabbing was a flight manoeuvre in which the owls flew slightly sideways into the wind at an oblique angle so as not to hit it head on. The owls scuttled across the wind in much the same way a crab moves – not directly forwards but in this case taking the best advantage of a wind that was determined to smack them back. But now, by stealing a bit off the wind's edges, the owls could move forwards, although slowly. They had been doing a lot of crabbing since they had left the last hollow and something they thought could never happen had happened. Their windward wings had actually grown tired and even sore. But at least their wings weren't icing up.

Suddenly, there was a terrible roar. The owls felt themselves sucked sideways as if an icy claw had reached out to drag them. There was another roar and they felt themselves smash into a wall of ice. Soren began sliding down a cold, slick surface. "Hang on, Mrs Plithiver," he called, but he had no sense of her nestling in her usual place. It was impossible to grab anything with his talons. His wings simply would not work. He felt himself going faster than he had ever flown. But something huge and grey and faster whizzed by him. Was it Twilight? No time to think. No time to feel. It was as if his gizzard had been sucked right out of him along with every hollow bone. But then he finally stopped. He was dazed, breathless, but mercifully

"What do you mean – *you guess, face?*" the creature hollered. "I mean, we're pretty dumb, but you must be dumber if you can't tell a face from a plant."

"Well, you look a bit like a cactus in bloom – the kind we have in the desert," Digger said.

"That's my beak, idiot. I can assure you that neither I nor anyone in my family is a cactus in bloom – whatever a cactus is and whatever a desert is."

"Well, what are you?" Mrs Plithiver finally spoke up.

"Well, what in the name of ice are you?" the creature retorted.

"I'm a snake... a nest-maid snake. I serve these most noble of birds, owls."

"Well," said the creature who was not a cactus, "we're just a bunch of puffins."

"Puffins!" Twilight hooted. "Puffins are northern birds, far northern birds."

"Duh!" said one of the little ones. "Gee, Pop, I'm feeling smarter all the time."

"But if you're puffins," Gylfie continued, "we must be in the North."

"Ta-da!" said one of the puffins. "Gee, you owls are getting smarter every minute!"

"Does she get a prize, Mummy, for answering the question right?" Another little chick, with an immense beak almost as long as it was tall, poked its head out of the hole.

"Oh, we're just having fun with them, Dumpy."

"But how did we get so far north?" Soren asked.

"Must have been blown off course," said the female. "Where you come from?"

"The Beaks," Twilight said.

"Where you headed?"

"The island in the Sea of Hoolemere."

"Great Ice! You've passed it by. Overshot it by five hundred leagues."

"What! We flew over it and didn't even see it?" Digger said, his voice barely audible.

"Where are we exactly?" Gylfie asked.

"You're in the Ice Narrows, far side of Hoolemere, edge of the Northern Kingdoms."

"What!" All four owls gasped.

"Don't feel too dumb," the male said. "Bad weather conditions."

"When do we ever have good ones, dear?" his mate mused.

"Well, true. But with the wind coming from that direction, they just got sucked up into the Narrows and then that williwaw came."

"What's a williwaw?" Soren asked.

"You get a big tumble, like an avalanche. Suppose you don't know what that is – an avalanche."

"No, what's an avalanche?" Digger said.

"You know, a big snow slide, but it's not snow in a williwaw. Just cold icy air comes over the wall and crashes down. That's what sucked you up into the Narrows and slammed you into our wall – our home."

"This is home?" Twilight asked.

"Yes, sir. Only one we've ever known," the male said.

"But where do you live?"

"In the ice cracks and some rocky holes. The wall is not all ice. Plenty of boulders. There are places if you know how to find them," he said and then looked at his mate. "Another storm is coming in from the south. We'd better get you owls inside. Follow us."

The ice nest was roomy, but it reeked something horrible. "What's that smell?" Gylfie whispered.

"What smell?" asked the little puffin they called Dumpy.

"That smell!" Digger snorted.

"Probably fish," the male said.

"Fish! You eat fish?"

"Not much else. Better get used to it."

"And I'm going fishing before that storm comes," the female said.

As she waddled towards the nest opening, Soren began to appreciate how truly preposterous this bird was. It was not only her face, with its large bulbous orange beak and the dark eyes ringed in red and set in slightly skewed ovals of white feathers, but also her body was the strangest shape. Chubby, with not one slim or graceful line and, with her chest thrust out, she appeared as if she might topple forwards at any second. How this thing flew was a mystery.

Indeed now, tottering on the edge of the nest, it appeared as if she hesitated to take off, but finally she did by windmilling her wings awkwardly until, at last, she seemed to organise them for a direct plunge into the sea. And that was something to behold. She suddenly grew sleek. Her broad head and thick beak split the icy turbulent waters, which then closed over her tail feathers. She completely disappeared beneath the surface. Soren had been joined by Twilight, Digger and Gylfie at the edge of the nest. They waited and waited, then looked at one another.

"Sir," Gylfie began, "I think something might have happened to your mate... uh... er... she dived into the sea and no sign of her yet."

"Oh, she'll be a while. Lot of mouths to feed."

It seemed like forever, but then they saw her break through the surface. Several small fish hung neatly from her beak. "There she is! There she is!" Gylfie said.

"Good old Ma," Dumpy sighed. "Hope she brought some capelin. I just love capelin. If you don't like it, will you give me yours? Please, please, please?"

"Sure," Soren said. Every minute that he stayed in this smelly hollow he was getting less hungry.

"Look at that," Twilight said. "How's she going to take off?" The others now crowded to the edge of the ice hollow. Down below, it appeared that the female was trying to run across the surface of the water while madly flapping her wings.

"Water take-off – not easy for any of us. We're not the best fliers, but, as you can see, we can dive. Got these little air pockets so we can go really deep for a long, long time. Getting back to the nest is the hardest part for us."

The male stepped out of the ice hollow and called down. "Dearest, try that patch over there under the lee, the water is smoother."

She gave her mate a withering glance, and somehow through the mouthful of fish yelled back, "You want me to fly directly into the wall, Puff Head? There's a tailwind. I'll slam beak-first into it. Then where will your dinner be? If you're so smart you come down and go fishing yourself."

"Oh, sorry dear, silly me." Then he turned to the owls. "We're really not that bright. I mean we dive well, know how to fish and deal with ice, but that's about it."

But in fact, the puffins knew more and were not that dumb at all. "Just low self-esteem," Gylfie said. The puffins, in addition to knowing how to dive and fish, knew weather. And just now they were telling them that there would be a small pocket of time when the wind would turn, and they could leave before the next storm came in.

"You see, young'uns," said the male puffin, "nine days out of ten, the wind slams full force up these Ice Narrows. That's how you got sucked into here in the first place. But on the tenth day, it can turn round and suck you right back out. Nice high stream coming through that could pull you right back to The Beaks, if you want to go that far." He paused and each of the owls stole a glance at one another. The Beaks sounded lovely. This place was so harsh and cold and there was the terrible stench of the fish and the awful oiliness that seemed to make their gizzards greasy. How could they help but think of the Mirror Lakes, where it was always summer and the voles were fat and the flying spectacular? They would be liars if they said they weren't tempted.

"So when should we leave?" Soren asked.

"I think since you owls like night flying you should go tonight. Just when it's getting dark is when the wind will begin to turn. It'll be easy flying out of here, and then when the wind finally gets behind your tail feathers, you'll really go, straight out to Hoolemere."

"But the blizzard?" Gylfie said. "When will that start up again?"

"Not before tomorrow, I think, at the earliest."

"We should all get some rest now," Soren said. "If we're going to fly tonight."

"Good idea," Mrs Plithiver nodded.

"Better go to the back of the hollow," the female puffin called. "Sun's coming out and it reflects so brightly off the ice you won't be able to shut your eyes against it." It was dimmer in the back, but still rather bright as streams of sunlight, bouncing off the ice-sheathed rocks, pried into the shadows of the hollow.

Soren could hear the steady drip as some of the ice began to melt. But finally he fell asleep. Perhaps it was the melting ice that made him think of that warmer place with the pools of crystal-clear water, his lovely white face shimmering on the surface. Why couldn't they go back there? Where were they supposed to be going instead? Soren kept forgetting. All he could remember were the rolls of warm wind to play on, the still, glass-like lake, the everlasting summer. No ice, no blizzard. Why not live there happily ever after? The dream tugged on him. In his sleep, he felt his gizzard turn and something begin to dim, while the longing for The Beaks and the Mirror Lakes grew stronger and stronger.

"Time to get up, young'uns." It was the male puffin, nudging Soren with one of his large, orange, webbed feet. "Wind died down. You can fly out of here now. The wall's weeping."

"Huh?" Soren asked. "What do you mean the wall's weeping?"

"The ice is melting. Means warm air, the thermals have come. Easy flying."

The other owls were already up and standing at the rim of the hollow. The wall certainly was weeping. Glistening with wetness, it appeared shimmering, almost fiery as the setting sun turned its ice into liquid flames of pink, then orange and red.

"Dumpy," his father called. "Come over here, son. I want you to step up here and watch the young'uns fly. They are the masters of silent flight. Never going to hear a wing flap with these owls!"

Just before they took off, Soren looked at each of the owls. He wasn't the only one who had dreamed of the Mirror Lakes. They all wanted to go back. Could it be that wrong if they all wanted to do it? Twilight slid in close to him. "Soren, the three of us have been thinking."

"Yes?"

"Thinking about The Beaks and the Mirror Lakes. We've been thinking, why not go back there for just a little while? You know, just to kind of rest up, get this fish out of our system. Eat us some nice fat voles, then go on to the Great Ga'Hoole Tree."

It was so tempting, so very tempting. Soren felt Mrs Plithiver shift in the feathers between his shoulders.

"I... I..." Soren stammered. "I think there's a problem."

"What's the problem?" Twilight pressed.

"I think that if we go there, we won't go on – ever – to the Great Ga'Hoole Tree," Soren replied.

Twilight paused. "Well, what if some of us think – you know, kind of differently? Would that be wrong of us to go? I mean, you'd be free to go on."

After they took off, Soren could feel Gylfie flying nervously beside him. He turned and looked directly at Gylfie. Together they had survived moon blinking and moon scalding. Together they had escaped St Aggie's. He spun his head towards Twilight and

Digger. They had fought with him and Gylfie in the desert and together killed the murderers of Digger's brother and parents. It was in that desert stained with blood that the four of them had, within the slivers of time and the silver of moonlight, sworn an oath and become a band. And it was as a band they had sworn to go to Hoolemere and find its Great Ga'Hoole Tree. That was no dream. That was real. But it was a dream that now threatened them, a dream of the Mirror Lakes and endless summer that could, in fact, destroy their reason for living.

Twilight continued, "I mean, Soren, as I said, you could go on if you wanted. What would be wrong with each of us doing what we want to do?"

Soren looked hard at Twilight. "Because we are a band," he said simply. And he sheered off towards an inlet near the end of the Ice Narrows that streamed into the Sea of Hoolemere.

CHAPTER SEVEN
This Side of Yonder

The puffins had told them that there was a current of darker green water that swirled out from the Ice Narrows, then curved into the Sea of Hoolemere and, if they followed it, it would lead them to the island. Soren was very thankful that they had found the current quickly. For although the other three owls seemed to understand what he had said about being a band, he did not know what he would have done if they hadn't found the current. At least for now he could assure them that they were on course. One more navigational error, one more time getting blown off in some wild direction – well, Soren wasn't sure if he could hold the band together. The draw of The

Mirror Lakes was powerful. It was odd, but he often thought of the night that he and Gylfie escaped from St Aggie's. When Skench, in her full battle regalia with claws and helmet, had burst in on them in the library, something had drawn her into the wall where the flecks were stored. She had actually slammed into the wall and become completely immobilised for a few brief seconds. But it had provided them with the time to escape. Somehow The Beaks and the Mirror Lakes had a similarly powerful draw for them. But it was just a dream and that is what Soren didn't understand. How could a dream do this? However, this current of dark green water beneath them was real. All they had to do was follow it.

They had been flying hard and fast for a while now. With each stroke of their wings, they felt surer of their course, and their gizzards began to tremble with excitement. And with each stroke that drew Soren closer to the island with the Great Ga'Hoole Tree, he knew he was flying somehow further away from St Aegolius Academy for Orphaned Owls. How dare they call that place an academy? For nothing was learned there. Indeed, one of the worst rules that an owl could break was that of asking a question. The most severe and the bloodiest punishments were reserved for questioners. The foulest words one could utter at St Aggie's were the cursed *wh* words: *what, when, why.* Soren at one point had all of his just-budging flight feathers ripped out and his wings left with a slick of blood because he had asked a question. Knowledge was forbidden.

Soon it began to snow, rubbing the pinpoints of starlight into smears, feathering the edges of the moon into a blurry softness and smudging the dark green line of the current. *I can't lose the current!* Soren thought.

"I don't know how we'll ever see this Island of Hoole," Digger said. "Look down. Everything is turning white."

"Where's the current?" asked Gylfie anxiously.

Soren felt Mrs Plithiver shift nervously in his neck feathers. *So near but so far!* They couldn't lose the current now. Soren thought that the Island of Hoole and the Great Ga'Hoole Tree seemed almost like the sky did to Mrs Plithiver, the Yonder. And right now it felt as if they were just this side of the Yonder.

The conditions became increasingly confusing for the owls to fly in. Accustomed in night flying to opening up their pupils so wide that they nearly filled the entire size of their eyes, on this snowy night the owls had to do the reverse and yet it was not like day flying. There was too much light and it was all the same colour, a shadowy grey. Water would appear no different from the surrounding land. Were they still over water? Or could they be over the Island of Hoole? Or maybe they had been blown off course again! Soren remembered what Mrs Plithiver had said, that one had to see with one's entire body. Mrs P's words came back to him. The four owls were bunched together in a tight V–shaped formation with Twilight at the point. Soren realised that flying on one side of the V or the other was not the best place to take advantage of the uneven placement of his ears and his good hearing.

"Let me fly point, Twilight. I'll be able to hear better."

Twilight slowed his speed and Soren stroked past him. "Hang on, Mrs P, I'm going to have to do some head rolls."

An owl's neck is a strange thing. Unlike most birds, owls have extra bones in their necks that allow them to swivel their heads far to each side, in an arc much wider than any other living creature. Indeed, an owl can flip its head back so that its crown touches its shoulders, or turn its face almost upside down as Soren was doing just now. "Hello!" said Soren to Mrs P, who nestled now directly beneath his beak as he flipped his face about. "Just scanning."

After several minutes of this, Soren noticed a change in the night. He was not sure exactly what it was but something seemed different. "Digger, remember that coyote song you were singing?"

"Yes."

"Sing it again and tip your head down."

"Hard to tell which way is down tonight."

Indeed it was, for the entire world, thick with snow, had suddenly turned completely white. But Digger began to sing in the thin grainy voice of a desert owl. Soren meanwhile was moving his head in small, minute movements. Finally he said, "I think we're still over water." The sound of Digger's song that was reflected back was different from when he had sung it when they were over land and his sound had disappeared into the softness of an earth clad with trees. Now the song came back sharp and crisp.

And then there came a moment when the wind died and the snowflakes seemed to stand still. Twilight spoke. "It's time for me to fly point again, Soren."

Soren knew he was right. The snowflakes had evaporated into a thick dense fog. The world, the water below, was shrouded in mist. It was time for the vision of Twilight – that time that Twilight had spoken about when Soren and Gylfie had first met him, that time that had given Twilight his name, when boundaries become dim and shapes begin to melt away. It was the time for the Great Grey Owl, who lived on the edges and saw invisible connections, the joinings in a world that had turned foggy and confusing. Maybe Twilight could find the current again.

Soren drifted back as the big owl stroked by him to the point position.

It seemed as if they had flown for hours since they had last seen the current. Gylfie was getting very tired and Digger's wing, the one injured by the crows, had begun to hurt. The wind was kicking up again and not in a favourable direction.

"I can't believe that a current can just disappear. The puffins said it would lead us right to the island," Soren muttered.

"What do they know?" Twilight hooted. "They even admit they're dumb."

"I don't think they're all that dumb," Soren said. "We've got to be able to find it."

"And there's no place to even fetch up out here and rest," Gylfie sighed.

"We got to go back," Twilight said.

"Go back where? Not to The Beaks," Soren spoke sharply.

"To any dry land. If The Beaks is the closest, then The Beaks it is," Twilight replied.

"No!" Soren said more fiercely. "Look, I'm going to fly down close to the water."

"That could be dangerous," Digger said. "Soren, that wind is kicking up big waves. You could be caught by one and believe me, I don't think you're the swimmer that the puffin was. You could be dragged right under."

"I'll be careful. Mrs P, if you want to slither on to Twilight, you can."

"No, dear, I'll stick with you. I'm not frightened."

"Good."

Soren began a banking turn down towards the water. Now, amid the blizzarding snow, the spume from the crests of waves spun up. How would he ever see a current in this mess? He flew lower. Still nothing. What if the others had flown off? Just given up. Could he truly blame them? He had the most dreadful feeling in his gizzard. What if he was left alone out here – just him and Mrs P?

Suddenly, Soren felt something stir in his gizzard. He said nothing but contracted and expanded his pupils. The world was absolutely white now. Oh, this was when he needed Twilight!

"Right here, Soren."

"Twilight! You followed me down."

"Call me a fool." Twilight peered into the whiteness, stretched, then shortened his actual eye tubes so that one second he was focusing near and the next far. Within the depths of the impenetrable white, Twilight saw two even whiter patches.

"Come, young'uns. You're right over the current. Can't tell it on a night like this, though. So, welcome to the Island of Hoole."

Two giant Snowy Owls had melted out from the night and they were so white that by comparison the mist seemed grey.

"I am Boron and this is my mate, Barran."

"You are the king and the queen of Hoole." Twilight whispered.

Digger and Gylfie, exhausted, plummeted down near them.

"Yes, my dears. But we prefer to be called teachers, or rybs. The word ryb means teacher and deep knowledge," said Barran.

"We're not keen on titles," chuckled Boron.

"But you came out to meet us?" said Soren.

"Of course," replied Boron. "You've done the hard part. Now let us guide you the rest of the way. It's not far."

The blizzard had been swallowed by the mist and the mist now seemed to melt away against the whiteness of Boron and Barran. The night turned black again and the stars broke out. As a half moon rose, the four young owls looked below and saw the vast sea glinting with silver spangles from the moonlight and then, directly ahead, spreading into the night, were the twisting branches of the largest tree they had ever seen, the Great Ga'Hoole Tree.

"We are here, Mrs Plithiver. We are here!" Soren whispered.

"I know, dear. I feel it. I feel it!"

The four young owls, led by Boron and Barran, threaded their way through the branches towards the centre of the tree where the opening of a hollow was revealed. Two Great Horned Owls held the moss curtains apart using their beaks as the young ones flew through. They alighted down inside. Soren thought that this hollow was not only huge but different from any other tree hollow he had ever seen, for it was light even though it was night. On the inside were strange flickering things.

Boron came up to Soren and the other three owls. "I see you have noticed our candles. You see, here in Hoole we have discovered how to capture fire and tame it for our own uses. You shall learn all about this, young ones. And who knows? One of you might even become a collier."

"A what?" asked Soren.

"A collier – a carrier of coals. It is a very special skill. But there are many skills you shall be able to learn here in the Great Ga'Hoole Tree and we are all here to teach you. These shall be your rybs."

With those words, Boron swept his wings towards the walls of the hollow. There were ledges that hung like galleries above. Soren, Twilight, Gylfie and Digger gasped as they saw a great gathering of owls – all kinds of owls from Burrowing ones to Barn Owls, from Pygmy Owls to Elf Owls, from Screech Owls to Sooty Owls, from Great Horned Owls to Snowy Owls. Every kind of owl imaginable was here within the hollow of the great tree, their yellow, black and amber eyes blinking and winking in the most friendly and inquisitive manner at the five new arrivals.

Barran continued, "Welcome, young ones. Welcome to the Great Ga'Hoole Tree. One journey has ended…"

Just one? thought Soren.

But just then a series of deep, rolling gongs began to shake the entire tree. Barran stopped mid-speech.

"Chaws – back up to your positions!" This hoot came from a Great Gry Owl in the gallery. Then, it seemed as if the entire hollow suddenly brightened as owls began donning battle claws and helmets, and the flames of the candles flickered off the bright polished surfaces of the armoured owls.

"Great Glaux – a battle! Quick, let's get our claws!" Twilight began to hop up and down, pumping his wings.

"Not so fast, young'un." A plump, Short-eared Owl waddled up to them.

"But where's the battle?" Twilight said.

"Beyond the Beyond." The Short-eared Owl fixed him in the glow of her amber gaze. "And it's not for you or you," she said, turning to Gylfie, "or you or you." She nodded to each one of the band. "And who are you?" She blinked at Mrs P.

"Mrs Horace Plithiver, nest-maid. I do have references."

"I see. Come along, all of you."

"But what about the battle?" Twilight sputtered.

"What about it? Not much really, just a skirmish on the borderlands between Silverveil and Beyond the Beyond."

CHAPTER EIGHT

First Night to First Light

They had begun by following the Short-eared Owl, known as Matron, through the enormous trunk of the Great Ga'Hoole Tree, which was honeycombed with passages of varying widths, all quite twisty and none that seemed to go in a straight line. Off the passageways there were hollows of different sizes. Some, it seemed, were for sleeping, others for study of some sort, some for stores and supplies. Soren peeked into one and saw stacks and stacks of the strange flickering things that Boron said were called candles. Sometimes Matron led them through a passage to the very end, where there might be a hole from which they would fly to another level of the tree, then re-enter through another opening and resume their interior trail through the trunk of the tree. As best as Soren could figure out, the sleeping quarters were closer to the top of the tree, meeting hollows for large and smaller congregations of owls seemed to be below, along with a hollow that was called a kitchen, from which very good smells issued. There were places along the way where small groups of owls gathered to socialise. These seemed to be near the points where some of the larger branches of the tree joined the trunk. There were good-sized openings at these points so that owls could either sit inside on specially constructed perches or outside on the branches themselves.

"Now, I want you young'uns to stay out of the way. We've got some wounded owls coming in and I have to arrange for their care." They were flying up through the branches, following the Short-eared Owl to the hollow that would be theirs.

"Matron, we're going to need moss and down. Search-and-rescue's coming in with two more little ones. Nest decimation." Another Short-eared Owl flew by with a wad of something fluffy in her talons.

"Oh, no! Poor little things."

"Nest decimation. What's that?" Soren asked.

"Accidental destruction of nests." A young Spotted

Owl flew up as they landed on a branch midway up the tree.

"Otulissa, thank goodness. Can you show these new arrivals to that hollow we cleaned out yesterday?"

"Certainly, Matron."

"And see if Cook has any tea or cakes left over. They look half starved."

"Certainly."

The Spotted Owl named Otulissa showed them to their hollow. "What is going on here?" Twilight asked her.

"Oh, there've been some skirmishes up in the borderlands, nothing too serious."

"Is it St Aggie's?" Soren asked. "We know all about St Aggie's. Gylfie and I escaped." Otulissa blinked.

"And we killed their top two lieutenants when they came after Digger here. So we're ready to fight," Twilight added. The Spotted Owl blinked again. "I mean, we're in the right place, aren't we? The Great Ga'Hoole Tree?" Twilight had stepped closer to the owl to ask his question.

"Where each night the order of knightly owls rises to perform noble deeds," Soren offered in a softer voice. An uncertain feeling that was not quite a doubt, yet not a real belief, began to stir in Soren's gizzard. "This is the place?" his voice quavered.

"Of course it's the place," the Spotted Owl replied.

"Then get us some battle claws – we're ready!" Twilight stomped one talon impatiently.

"You're ready!" Otulissa gasped. "You think just because you escaped and killed two rattlebrained owls, you're ready?"

"And the bobcat," Soren said.

"And the crows," Digger piped up. "Well, not exactly killed them, but drove them off."

Gylfie was very still, however. She had said nothing. But now the Elf Owl stepped forwards. "Are you trying to tell us we are not ready... that... that it takes more?"

"Indeed. There is nothing that noble about slaughtering two bad owls in the desert." The Spotted Owl rose up to her full height and looked down her beak at Gylfie. In a very haughty voice she said, "You have not been tempered by battle yet. Nor do you know the first thing about strategy. You probably don't even know how to fly with battle claws. I have been here much longer than you and still have not yet become a member of a chaw."

"What's a chaw?" Soren said.

"You are selected to join a chaw – a small team of owls – and you will learn a skill that is helpful."

"In battle?" Twilight asked.

"Not just battle – in life. There is more to life than

just battles. Each chaw has its own, oh, how should I put it? Personality. Navigation chaw tends to have a kind of elegance, they are all superb flyers, as are the members of search-and-rescue, but they, of course, are less refined. Weather interpretation and colliering are decidely rough and uncouth. But," and the Spotted Owl fixed a very intense gaze on Twilight, "they are all fiercely brave and can fight or fly to the death!"

Twilight seemed to swell in anticipation, but Soren almost shrank with fear. Would he be up to it? He had to be. With his friends, he could. Look what they had accomplished so far! "Do we all get to be in the same chaw?" Soren asked.

"Probably not."

"But we're a band." Soren hoped that he did not sound as if he were pleading.

"That doesn't matter now. You're part of a larger band. I have to go."

"Duty calls, I suppose," Gylfie said with a slight edge in her voice.

"I suppose it does." Otulissa again looked down at the Elf Owl, then she left the hollow. Soren thought Gylfie was going to spit at her.

"I don't like her one bit," Twilight said.

"Me neither. Did you see how she looked at me? She might think she's all hoity-toity and very refined, but I bet she makes tasteless stature jokes all the time." Gylfie was very sensitive, like many Elf Owls, about remarks concerning size and shortness. Her grandmother had been a founder of SOS – the Small Owl Society – whose purpose was to prevent cruel and tasteless remarks about size.

"Make way! Make way!" Just outside their hollow, they saw two burly Great Horned Owls flying by, carrying a hammock with another owl collapsed on it. The wounded owl's helmet was askew and one wing drooped off the edge of the hammock at an odd angle.

Then, through the walls of the hollow, Soren thought he heard the mewling sound of a young crying owl and another voice saying, "There there." Soren crept out of an opening leading into an inner passageway that wound through the trunk. There were many of these passageways and it seemed to Soren that one might get hopelessly lost. But he began to follow the sound. Soon he came to another hollow. Like most, this hollow had both an inside and an outside entrance so that one could either fly in or walk in from one of the many inner pathways through the trunk of the tree. He peeked in. He saw the Short-eared Owl called Matron who had led them to their own hollow. She was bustling about, plucking down from her own breast and tucking it in around an owl. "Now, now, dear, we know you did your best."

"But what will Mum and Da think?" For a moment Soren's gizzard gave a lurch. Could this little owl be Eglantine?

"They will think that you were a brave little Pygmy Owl," Matron replied.

Soren sighed.

"What are you doing out there? Don't just stand around, come in and make yourself useful," Matron called. Soren came slowly into the hollow. The little owl was nearly as small as Gylfie; she was very fluffy, although she smelled of soot and some of her feathers were singed. "Now what did you say your name was, dear?" Matron bent over the Pygmy Owl.

"Primrose."

"Yes. Primrose here lost her nest."

"The whole tree," gulped the little owl.

"Yes, indeed. See, her parents had gone off to fight in the borderlands skirmishes, and they had left her all safe and sound."

"I was supposed to be sitting the two new eggs. Mum was really only off hunting, not fighting. She was going to be right back."

"What happened?" Soren asked.

"A fire – forest fire. I didn't think it would reach our tree and when it did, well, I tried to save one of the eggs. But you know, I haven't been flying that long and, well, I just..." Here, she began to sob uncontrollably.

A bunchy Barred Owl poked her head in. "Any tea here?"

"Oh, yes, I think a cup of milkberry tea would be lovely."

"I dropped the egg. I don't deserve to live." Primrose emitted a long sound halfway between a whistle and a wail.

"Don't say that!" Soren exclaimed. "Of course you deserve to live. Every owl deserves to live. That's why we came here."

Matron stopped what she was doing and cocked her head and regarded the young Barn Owl. Perhaps he was learning; just perhaps he was beginning to catch a glimmer of the true meaning of a noble deed. She would leave him to comfort this little Pygmy Owl and send in an extra cup of tea and some milkberry tart.

Soren stayed with Primrose for the rest of the evening. She was sometimes a bit feverish and would begin to mumble about the little brother she was sure she had killed. She had wanted to call him Osgood. Other times, she was quite lucid and would blink and say to Soren, "But what about Mum? What about Da? What will they think when they come home and find our forest burned, our tree gone? Will they look for me?"

And Soren simply did not know how to answer her, for indeed he had asked himself the same question so many times. Near daybreak, Primrose was sound asleep and Soren decided to make his way back to his own hollow. He meandered through the central hollow of the tree and more than once took a wrong turn that led down another passageway. While wandering down a particularly twisty one, he met up with an elderly Spotted Owl.

"Ah, one of the new arrivals, part of that band that flew in from the Ice Narrows," she hooted softly.

"Yes, well, we don't come from the Narrows. We were blown off course. We'd left from The Beaks but somehow..."

"Oh dear... yes, The Beaks, only for the strongest gizzards."

Soren blinked. Now what did she mean by that?

"I'm Strix Struma. Perhaps you need to sharpen your navigational skills: I am the navigation ryb. It's getting to be First Light, so I suggest you hasten to your hollow. And if you are very quiet, you shall hear the music of Madame Plonk's harp. It is lovely to go to sleep to and she has a fine voice."

"What's a harp? What's music?" Soren asked. He remembered the awful songs of St Aggie's. Surely this must be different.

"Oh, dear. It's hard to explain. Listen and you'll begin to know."

When he got back to his hollow, they were all having cups of milkberry tea. "It's amazing, Soren," Gylfie said. "Nest-maid snakes brought the tea around on their backs."

"Yes, I really think there will be a place for me here, Soren. I think I can serve." Mrs P almost glowed as she said the word.

Everyone seemed quite content except for Twilight. "I didn't kill those two fiends of St Aggie's, I didn't battle crows and tear out the throat of a bobcat to sit on my tail feathers and be served tea." Twilight seemed to swell to twice his size.

"Well, what can you do, Twilight?" Gylfie said.

"I think we have to have a word with the head owls – Boron and Barran. I don't think they know what real evil is. This border skirmish up there that they are talking about – it has nothing to do with St Aggie's. You heard what little Miss Stuck-up Spotted Owl said. I don't think they know what they're in for. But we do!" He slid his yellow eyes about the hollow. "Right?"

"You mean the 'you only wish'?" Digger whispered the words of the dying Barred Owl. They had never really spoken about the meaning of those words, but they knew that the Barred Owl had meant, in no uncertain terms, that there was something out there that was far worse than St Aggie's.

"Yes," Soren said hesitantly. "Maybe we should go talk to the king and queen. But not now. It's daylight. Time to sleep."

The hollow was lined with the finest mosses and the fluffiest down. Soren made his way to a corner near the opening to watch the breaking dawn. The very last of the evening stars was just winking out and a lovely pinkness began to spread in the sky. The immense gnarled limbs of the Great Ga'Hoole Tree stretched out and seemed to embrace the new day.

"This down," Soren whispered to Mrs Plithiver, "reminds me of Mum."

"Oh, doesn't it, dear!" said Mrs Plithiver, arranging herself into a neat coil in the same corner. Then, as the owls nestled down, the loveliest, most unearthly sounds began to pling softly through the Great Ga'Hoole Tree, and a voice began to sing.

Night is done, gone the moon, gone the stars
From the skies.
Fades the black of the night
Comes the morn with rosy light.
Fold your wings, go to sleep,

Rest your gizzards,
Safe you'll be for the day.
Glaux is nigh.
Far away is First Black,
But it shall seep back
Over field
Over flower
In the twilight hour.
We are home in our tree.
We are owls, we are free.
As we go, this we know
Glaux is nigh.

Soren never remembered feeling so peaceful.

"Digger, Soren, Gylf, you asleep?" Twilight called.

"Almost, Twi," Digger and Soren replied.

"How long do you think until we get our battle claws?"

"I have no idea, Twilight. But don't worry, good light," Soren replied sleepily.

"Good light, Twi," Digger said.

"Good light, Soren," Gylfie said.

"Good light, Gylf," Soren replied. And then added. "Good light, Mrs Plithiver."

But Mrs Plithiver was already sound asleep.

CHAPTER NINE

A Parliament of Owls

The four owls were in the antechamber of another hollow called the parliament. They were waiting to be admitted for their meeting with Boron and Barran.

"Very important business inside, young'uns," an owl on guard spoke in the soft *tings* of a Boreal Owl.

"We won't take long," Gylfie said.

I hope not, thought Soren. He was frightened. The other three had decided that he should be the one to speak.

Another owl stuck her head out. "You can come in now. But be quiet and wait your turn."

She indicated a branch where they should perch. Soren looked about. It was not an especially large hollow, not nearly as big as the one in which they had first been welcomed by Boron and Barran. There were candles, of course, and there was one long white branch from a tree that Soren thought was called a birch that had been bent into a half circle. It was on this white branch that the owls of the parliament, no more than a dozen, perched. He recognised the elderly Strix Struma, the Spotted Owl he had met the night before. She perched next to a Great Horned Owl of an unusual ruddy colour with even more unusual very black talons. Then there was an ancient and decrepit Whiskered Screech, who appeared to have the worst case of feather fletch Soren had ever seen. Not that he had seen all that many. The Whiskered Screech had a long bristly beard. One of his eyes seemed stuck in a perpetual squint, and his beak had a notch in it.

"I've never seen a more disreputable-looking owl," Gylfie whispered. "Great Glaux, look at his foot! His talons!" She paused. "Or lack of!" The Whiskered Screech, indeed, had only three talons on one foot. And just as Soren was blinking in a mixture of astonishment and horror, the old owl swung his head about and fixed Soren in his squinted gaze. Soren thought his gizzard was going to drop right out of him.

"So, Elvanryb," Boron turned and addressed another owl, a Great Grey. "It is your notion that we need to have a search-and-rescue attachment chaw on the colliering missions?"

"Not all missions, Boron. I think they are only necessary when we are in areas near battle zones. So often the parents are off fighting. In normal circumstances, the parents are there if a fire breaks out but tonight, for instance, we had to pick up that little Pygmy and a Northern Saw-whet. We got them back but it taxed our chaw, believe me – carrying coals and injured owlets. Can't exactly drop them in the coal bucket. And I don't even like to think of the ones we might have missed and left behind."

The old Whiskered Screech raised his deformed foot.

"Yes, Ezylryb?" Boron nodded to the owl.

"Question for Bubo." the Whiskered Screech's voice was a low growl. "You think this fire was natural or more trouble with the rogue raids?"

"No telling, sir. The rogues make good targets, and it wouldn't be the first time raiding one caused a fire."

"Hmmm," the Whiskered Screech replied, and then scratched his head with the second of the three remaining talons of one foot.

"Next order of business," Boron said. "Something about starvation in Ambala?"

Ambala! Soren and Gylfie looked at each other. Ambala was where their friend the great Hortense came from. When they had first met Hortense at St Aggie's, they thought she was the most perfectly moon-blinked creature ever. Moon blinking was perhaps the cruelest thing that St Aggie's did to young owls. By forcing them to sleep during the full shines of the moon, directly exposing their heads to the moon's light, they destroyed the will, the very personalities of individual owls and made them perfectly obedient with no thoughts of their own. Soren and Gylfie had devised a plan for fooling the sleep monitors and escaping the full shine. It turned out so had Hortense. She, in fact, was an infiltrator and had been sneaking out the eggs that St Aggie's patrols had been snatching. Unfortunately, she was caught and killed. Still, they had heard that Hortense had become a legend in Ambala because of her heroic deeds.

"Yes," another owl was speaking now. "The egg production is down and it is thought to be caused by a blight on the rodent population. Simply not enough food." Soren and Gylfie exchanged looks. It was not just the rodent population. It was the St Aggie's egg snatchers. This was information they could offer. This might convince Boron and Barran that they really knew something.

"We'll look into it," Boron said. "And now, I believe some of our new arrivals have requested to speak with us." He turned and blinked at the four young owls.

Speak with us! What was he talking about? Soren was not prepared to talk in front of all these owls.

"Now who wants to go first?"

Twilight, Digger, and Gylfie all looked at Soren.

"Up here, young'un." There was a perch in the middle of the half circle to which Boron nodded.

Oh, my Glaux. I have to fly up and stand there all by myself. Soren was so much more comfortable sharing this lower perch with his friends. Great Glaux, he would be close enough to that weird owl Ezylryb to reach out and touch his three-taloned foot. Soren got a terrible queasy feeling, not in his gizzard but in his first stomach, the one before the gizzard. How embarrassing if something just came up out of his gullet and went *splat.*

"Uh... my name is Soren. I am from the Forest of Tyto. I, er..." He and Gylfie had discussed how he should explain the events leading up to his snatching by St Aggie's. Gylfie felt it was not good to go into too much detail about Kludd actually shoving him from the nest. "Tales of attempted fratricide might not be the right way to start," Gylfie had said.

Of course, Soren hadn't known what fratricide was until Gylfie explained it meant killing your brother. Then he agreed with her. He certainly didn't want the owls of the Great Ga'Hoole Tree to think he came from such a murderous family. Kludd was the only one, after all. "I was snatched by a St Aggie's patrol. It was at St Aggie's that I met Gylfie."

It was difficult at first to speak and not look at Ezylryb's mangled foot, but as he spoke, Soren became more relaxed. The owls seemed attentive but not particularly impressed, not even when he told them about Hortense and that it was not simply starvation that was accounting for the low egg counts in Ambala.

"And so?" Barran said when Soren appeared to have concluded.

"And so what?" Soren asked.

"What is it you want, dear?"

"The four of us are a band. We have flown together, fought together and escaped many dangers – as a band. We know from our experience that there is great evil that threatens every owl in every owl kingdom on earth. We want only to fight this evil, to become guardian knights of this order." He saw Ezylryb stifle a yawn and pick up what appeared to be a dried caterpillar to munch. "We feel that we have special knowledge. We have much to offer," Soren concluded.

"I am sure you do," said Boron. "Every owl here has special knowledge and during your training you will find out what your talents are. You will, after proper instruction, be chosen for a chaw and then your learning will advance to a higher level, become more specialised." He explained why they probably would not be put into the same chaws, even though they were a band. "We do not all need to learn the same things. Each of you will make your band better in the end if you learn different skills. And this all takes time."

Soren felt Twilight rustle behind him. He knew it was Twilight without even flipping his head for a look. He also felt that the old owl, Ezylryb, despite his yawning and munching, was looking at him sharply. Indeed, he felt locked in that old owl's sights. He might as well be a mouse scuttling across a forest floor about to be pounced on by a bird of prey. It was as if that little scrap of amber that glimmered through the squinty eye had trapped him. He had never felt such a penetrating, piercing look and yet to the other owls of the parliament it did not appear as if Ezylryb was regarding him at all. Rather, it seemed as if he was bored silly with the young Barn Owl.

Boron continued to speak, "It takes time, of which I

think you have an abundance. It takes patience – of that, I am not sure how much you have – and, most important, it takes dedication and that, young'un, is found both in the heart and the gizzard. The nobility of the owls you see here in the parliament has not simply been given, nor has it been earned through courageous acts. Indeed, nobility is not always found in the flash of battle claws or flying through the embered wakes of firestorms, or even in making strong the weak, mending the broken, vanquishing the proud, or making powerless those who abuse the frail."

Soren's gizzard grew quiet as Boron spoke. "It is also found in the resolute heart, the gizzard that can withstand the temptations of false dreams, the mind that has the imagination to comprehend another's pain, as I think one young owl did tonight when he sat by the little Pygmy Owl with quiet understanding of her loss of tree, nest, family and egg. It is all of this that ultimately confers nobility and makes the Guardians of Ga'Hoole rise in the night with hearts sublime." Boron paused and looked at the other three owls. "And so as I said when you arrived, one journey has ended and now another starts. On the night of the morrow your training shall begin."

CHAPTER TEN

Twilight on the Brink

Dawn is the thief of night, and the night is when owls stir and become alive, when they fly. So the day that follows that dawn is only for sleeping, to prepare for the night. For some, however, the day feels like an eternity. And for the four young owls the night to come, the morrow night of their training, was still hours away.

Perhaps it had been a mild twinge in Soren's gizzard or a faint stirring in his heart, but sometime near midday, while the hollow was thick with sleep, the young Barn Owl sensed that something was slightly amiss, perhaps incomplete. It was not the feeling of dreadful cold fear that could steal into one's gizzard and make one's wings go yeep. No, not that at all, but something was not right. Soren's eyes blinked open, and in the dim milky light of the day that filtered into the hollow he saw only two other owls. Twilight was gone!

Soren blinked again. Was he really gone? In the flick of a wing, Soren had lofted onto the rim of the hollow. Every limb of the Great Ga'Hoole Tree stood out keen and black against the dull winter sky. Shadows were cast with sharp edges. There was, however, one long shadow stretched between the thick, gnarled branches of the tree, swelling like a dark cloud dropped down from above. That shadow was Twilight's. The Great Grey was perched on one of the less public take-off branches. Soren flew up.

"What are you doing, Twilight?" Soren spoke softly.

"Thinking."

That was a good sign. Twilight was a creature of action, of instinct. Not to say that the Great Grey Owl was stupid. He just acted out of an incredibly honed instinct and rarely meditated. "Thinking of leaving," Twilight added in a flat, dull voice.

"Leaving?" Soren was stunned. "But we're a band, Twilight."

"We're not a band, Soren. Boron and Barran said as much."

"They didn't exactly say we're not a band, Twilight."

"I think that is exactly what they meant. They said it was highly unlikely that any of us would be chosen for the same chaw. They said it was not the Ga'Hoolian way. In other words, they are separating us."

"They are separating us only for the chaws and that's because they want us all to learn different things. That doesn't mean we're not a band. A band isn't just perching side by side, or even flying side by side all the time."

Twilight blinked. "Well, what is it, then?"

Soren paused. This was hard. Maybe he wasn't quite sure what a band was. But no, that wasn't right. In his gizzard he knew they were a band. "We are a band despite what any owl says or does. In our gizzards, we are a band and we feel that. It cannot be undone. We are what we are and I know it and you know it and we all know it – even they know it."

Twilight dropped his eyelids so that they were only glinting slits of gold.

He's going to tell me about the Orphan School of Tough Learning. I just know it, Soren thought.

But Twilight didn't. "I am an owl of low birth in the eyes of the world because I have had no proper upbringing." All the bluster was gone from Twilight's voice; even his feathers seemed to sag a bit and he appeared slightly smaller. "I have had no First Ceremonies, no First Insect, no First Fur-on-Meat ceremony. There is much I don't know."

Soren was stunned. Twilight never admitted to not knowing anything.

"But there is much I do know. I know light and shadow and everything in between. I know the life pulse in the throat of a bobcat and where to slash to break the blood pump that is the cat's heart. I know mountains and deserts and the creatures who fly and those who don't, but slither or crawl or leap. I know of all sorts of claws, as well as fangs and poisons that lock the talons and freeze the wings. I know the false horizon that comes in the heat of the summer when the air is thick with dew and confuses old owls so that they go yeep and fall. And I know all this not because I was reared in a hollow lined with the down of my mother's breast, but because I was not. I was alone within minutes of my hatching. I can be alone. It is a special talent. And I can be alone again."

Soren's gizzard twisted in slow dread. Twilight turned his head slowly and blinked. "But I also know that I am a better owl with you and with Gylfie and Digger. I know now that I am part of a band. And I know this because of you, Soren – you alone." The Great Grey paused and mused. The gold in his eyes seemed to grow softer, like that pale haze of yellow just above the horizon as the sun begins to set.

"Perhaps, Soren, you are the blood pump of the band, and I would not want to slash such a life pulse." Soren blinked. "You are right, Soren. We are a band. And nothing can or will undo it. We are our own guardians."

"And maybe someday we shall become the Guardians of Ga'Hoole," Soren said quietly.

So the two owls returned to the hollow for sleep and the day grew brighter and brighter. And finally the light began to seep away as the dull blue of the winter sky darkened. The clouds became tinged with purple and the last blaze of the sinking sun turned the horizon as red as the bobcat's blood. Then at last the stars broke out and it was time for the owls of Ga'Hoole to rise.

CHAPTER ELEVEN

The Golden Talons

It was the deep, black part of the night. The moon had passed through its last moment of the dwenking and now it was gone completely. Gone for two nights at least, until its first silvery thread would reappear at the newing. Soren had been at the Great Ga'Hoole Tree for almost a month, which meant thirty nights and one complete moon cycle from dwenking to newing. Yes, Soren knew how to count now. To count and much more, really. But counting was special. He remembered thinking that his father had said that the fir tree in which his family had their hollow was nearly ninety feet tall. But Soren had no idea what the number meant, just as he had no idea how long sixty-six days were, which was the length of time it took a Barn Owl, such as himself, to fledge flight feathers. Numbers had been meaningless and he had promised himself, once he had escaped from the awful St Aggie's, that he would learn how to count.

But there was so much more to learn than simply counting. For a month now, he had had many lessons – flying lessons, even work with battle claws. They had practised with almost every chaw except for the navigation chaw and the colliering and weather interpretation chaws. For the last chaw, weather, Soren had felt spared because it was led by the grizzled old Screech, Ezylryb. The members were considered among the fiercest and the bravest of the entire Great Ga'Hoole Tree, for they had to fly through all sorts of storms, blizzards and even hurricanes to gather important information for troops going into battle or on missions of search-and-rescue. And they brought back coals from burning forest fires, which fed the forge that made so many vital things for the Great Ga'Hoole Tree, from battle claws to pots and pans, and, of course, gave light to the candles.

And now on this blackest of nights, he was learning to navigate from Strix Struma.

"We shall begin with a few simple tracing exercises," Strix Struma had announced when they were poised on the main take-off branch of the Great Ga'Hoole Tree. "The Great Glaux will soon rise," she continued. "The time of the Little Raccoon has, of course, passed by this season but a new beauty shall appear for the first time tonight. The Golden Talons. It is an unusual constellation, for in this part of the world it shall be with us through summer." She raised her foot from the branch. "And just like our talons, there are four – long, curved, and sharp ones formed by the stars."

"But not gold," piped up Primrose, the Pygmy Owl that Soren had befriended on the night she had been brought in from the borderlands, singed and orphaned.

"The gold is an illusion, my dear," Strix Struma said. "It is caused by atmospheric wobble, which you shall learn more about."

With a sudden blur and a slicing sound through the air, Strix Struma's talons shot out and caught a fruit bat on the wing. "A little snack before we fly," she said and quickly de-winged it, then served up tasty morsels to the class. "We don't want to overeat before our lesson. That is never good, but a bit of bat gives a boost, I always find. Now, ready!"

"Yes, Strix Struma," they all replied.

Strix Struma preferred to dispense with the title of ryb and instead be called by her family name. She was a Spotted Owl who came from a very ancient ancestry of which she was intensely proud. "Good, then. Primrose, I would like you flying directly behind me. Otulissa, seeing as you have had navigation class before, I think I shall put you on my windward flank. Gylfie, you shall fly in the downwind flanking position. And Soren, you fly tail. Any questions?"

Soren blinked in amazement. Although he had been at the Tree a month, those two simple words, 'any questions', were still like magic to him after St Aggie's.

Strix Struma always used the battle terminology, such as 'flanks'. For not only did Strix Struma have a proud and ancient lineage, but she had been trained for combat as a windward flanking sub-commander and had seen action at the Battle of Little Hoole. "Off we go, then!" And the large Spotted Owl rose in flight with the four young owls quickly manoeuvring into their positions.

Soren flew several lengths behind Strix Struma so as not to be affected by the eddies curling off her very broad tail. He wished Twilight and Digger were flying with them but Twilight was in a more advanced navigation class. And Digger was still in power-flight school due to his weak flying skills.

Twilight's orphan school of tough learning had apparently taught him a lot because he had been placed in many advanced classes.

"All right, class." Strix Struma spoke in the broad hooting tones that were indeed the voice of a mature Spotted Owl. These hoots now rolled back towards Soren. "Two points off to windward. Please note the first star of the Golden Talons rising."

"Ooooh, this is sooooo exciting." It was Otulissa trying her best to sound exactly like Strix Struma, which she would someday, for she too was a Spotted Owl. But right now, she just sounded like what she was – a beak-polishing, feather-fluffing idiotic owl always trying to impress the rybs. "And it's such an honour to be flying windward flank, Strix Struma, in the grand tradition of your noble family."

Soren blinked and winced. If Twilight had been here he would have yarped a pellet mid-flight right in her face. Soren saw Glyfie spin her head back and blink as she moved her beak silently. But Soren could understand perfectly what she was saying: "Can you believe her?"

Primrose spoke up. "Do you have a cold, Otulissa? You sound clogged up."

Oh, great Glaux. Soren thought he might die laughing. Leave it to Primrose! And the best part of it was that she was sincere. Primrose never suspected anyone of anything. "Guileless," Gylfie called her. "Charmingly guileless." Often Soren didn't understand the words that Gylfie used, but in this case he began to. He knew what Gylfie meant. Primrose didn't have a fake hollow bone in her body. She was utterly truthful and always believed that owls were motivated by the best of reasons. She had, needless to say, never spent any time at St Aggie's.

The navigation class flew on. It was not long after the first star in the Talons rose that several more broke out of the blackness, and it did seem as if four great golden talons clawed at the night.

"We shall trace each talon from its toe base to its sharp tip," hooted Strix Struma.

Soren was now flying directly behind Primrose, and he was becoming slightly confused as she constantly swivelled her head. An oddity about Pygmy Owls was that they had two dark spots on the back of the head that indeed looked like eyes. Soren was finding this disorientating.

"Confusing isn't it, dear?" Strix Struma had dropped back. "You're in a difficult position behind Primrose, but it's good training."

"Oh, Soren." Primrose swivelled her head. "It's my spots, isn't it? I'm so embarrassed."

"Nonsense, child!" Strix Struma hooted. "Don't you ever belittle those spots. You'll see, they'll come in handy someday. We must learn to use our Glaux-given gifts and in that way they truly become not just gifts but treasures. Now you fly on. You're doing a nice job and I shall teach Soren some tricks to reduce his disorientation.

"I had to fly behind a Pygmy for years. Made me a terrific navigator. Now, what you do, Soren, is you focus just below the spots. That will help you."

And it did. In no time the spots seemed to entirely vanish.

They flew on through the night, practising mostly by tracing the Golden Talons. But now, one by one, the stars of the constellations slipped away over some distant horizon and into another world, and Strix Struma led her class home to the Great Ga'Hoole Tree in the middle of the Sea of Hoolemere, which, in its own way, was another world as well.

CHAPTER TWELVE

Hukla, Hukla and Hope

There was the noisy chattering of young owls, which was known as gazooling. Soren remembered it from his brief few weeks with his own family in the old fir tree. His sister Eglantine, his brother Kludd and he would all try out their unformed voices in a range of hoots and shreeings. Barn Owls were more screamers than hooters. It was a raucous time of the day before getting ready to rest. Here at the Great Ga'Hoole Tree it was even rowdier. But for Soren, as the black of night thinned to grey and the grey became a cool purple that eventually warmed to rose, it could be a melancholy time.

Soren could not figure out why he felt so sad. He had a lot to gazool about, as much as anyone else. Of course,

Twilight came up to him first and Soren could barely squeeze in a word. "I did a fantastic power dive tonight. A tight spiral and I was down on the ground before you could flick a blink. Soren, I think Barran was really impressed. So you think there's a chance that she might recommend me for search-and-rescue?"

"But Twilight, if you were in the advanced navigation class with Barran why were you practising search-and-rescue moves?"

"Because Barran also teaches search-and-rescue. She is the one who taps for the search-and-rescue chaw."

That was all anyone ever talked about – being tapped for the various chaws. Next Otulissa came up. "Oh, I don't know, Twilight, about you getting tapped for search-and-rescue chaw. Don't get your hopes up. They tend to take owls with very old family lines. Those ranks are almost always reserved for Strix, just like navigation."

"Oh, racdrops!" boomed Bubo. "Make way! Make way! Let the nest snakes serve tea. We all be starving and don't need to listen to none of this nonsense about old family lines. It's what you do here and now on this earth that counts."

Bubo was the ruddy-coloured owl with the very black talons whom Soren had first seen in the parliament. A high-shouldered, enormous Great Horned Owl, his ear tufts alone stood as tall as Gylfie. His plumage was of an unusual colouring for a Great Horned, most of whom tended towards the brownish-grey tones. Bubo's feathers were actually almost flame-coloured, which seemed appropriate, as he headed up the forge and was the blacksmith. So despite what was said about Bubo's lowly origins and rough-and-tumble manner – a constant stream of curses issued from his beak – he was treated with great respect in the community of the Great Ga'Hoole Tree because he was an expert blacksmith. The discovery and the taming of fire was the single thing that most impressed Soren about the owls of the Great Ga'Hoole Tree.

"Line up! Line up! Now, please don't rush the dear snakes. Don't crowd the snakes by cramming in too many of you around one snake. Please proceed in an orderly fashion." It was Matron speaking, the Short-eared Owl. The nest-maid snakes began to slither into the dining hollow. These snakes were all blind like Mrs Plithiver. Gylfie, Soren, Twilight and Digger always lined up at Mrs Plithiver's table for she had been invited to join the staff and was thrilled to be in service once more.

The melancholy feelings that had filled Soren a

few minutes before disappeared as he and his friends stepped up to Mrs P's back.

"Hello, dearies," Mrs P hissed in her soft voice. "Good night in the Yonder? Classes went well?"

"Look!" Digger said. "Primrose over there doesn't have a place to sit."

"Sorry, Primrose," Otulissa was saying, "but this snake is all filled up." Otulissa was with four other young Spotted Owls.

"Over here, Primrose." Gylfie waved a wing. "We have a place."

"Always room, dearie," Mrs P said as Primrose came over. "I can always stretch myself a little longer and fit in another young one."

"Oh, thank you. Thank you so much," Primrose spoke in a shaky voice.

"You all right, Primrose?" Digger asked kindly.

"I'm fine. Just fine." She didn't sound all that fine. "Well, not so fine," she admitted. "All this talk of tapping is really making me nervous."

"Now, I believe there is entirely too much talk about this tapping business," Mrs P said. "I think you young ones should just drink your tea while it is still nice and warm. Cook made a special effort with the milkberries. I think she added a few extra as the season shall be coming again soon and perhaps she can spare more for tea without worrying."

"It's hard not to think about tapping, Mrs P," Soren said. "It's all anyone talks about."

"They say most Burrowing Owls like myself are tapped for tracking, since we have such strong legs and really know the countryside so well. I think I'd like that," Digger said quietly.

"I want search-and-rescue myself. You get to wear battle claws," Twilight spoke up.

"You want to fight?" Primrose said with a note of alarm in her voice.

"I'd like to fight any owl from St Aggie's. Let me tell you, we gave those two a run for it that time in the desert. Didn't we?" He blinked towards Soren and Gylfie. Soren and Gylfie both prayed that Twilight would not break into one of his dancing chants and shadow fights with an imaginary opponent in the dining hall. As much as they loved him, he could be really embarrassing.

"Thank goodness," sighed Digger. "If it hadn't been for them and of course the eagles, I would be dead." Digger paused. "Not just dead... eaten."

"You're joking?" Primrose gasped.

"I'm not joking," Digger said.

"Oh, come on, tell me the story," Primrose urged.

"Young ones, I don't think this is tea-table talk and since I *am* the tea table I would prefer not."

But it was too late. Digger had already launched into his story and Primrose was spellbound. Mrs Plithiver just sighed and muttered, "Hukla, hukla," which, in the special language of blind snakes, meant "young owls will be young owls".

Mrs Plithiver dozed off as the owls continued to talk and sip their cups of tea.

"So here's how the joke goes. You got a bunch of crows and other wet poopers like hummingbirds and seagulls." Twilight had begun telling a joke.

"Oh, yes. Seagulls are disgusting," Primrose offered.

"Definitely," Soren joined in. "They are disgusting."

"We should have a contest to see who can tell the slimiest wet poop joke," Digger said.

Suddenly, their little nut cups of tea trembled. "Enough is enough!" Mrs Plithiver screeched a hiss that curled through the air. "I shall not have this talk at the table. This is inappropriate on every level." Then her rosy scales shimmered with a new radiance and with one quick writhing motion all the teacups clattered off her back.

This was not the first time a nest-maid snake had shaken off teacups. There were not many rules at the Great Ga'Hoole Tree but, as Matron instructed the young owls, there were to be no wet poop jokes anywhere, and especially not in the dining hollow. Therefore the nest snakes were under orders, if it was teatime and they were serving, to immediately dismiss the culprits, and this was accomplished in just the manner Mrs P had done when she shook herself.

They were ordered to go and see Boron and Barran. As could be expected, Barran scolded them and told them that their behaviour was shocking. "Poor form," she called it. Boron kept muttering, "Don't be too hard on them, dear. They're just youngsters. Young males do that kind of thing."

"Boron, I would like to point out that Primrose and Gylfie are not males."

"Oh, but I still know a lot of wet poop jokes," Primrose tooted up.

The air was laced with the soft *churr* sounds that owls make when they laugh. They were all churring except for Barran. Boron was churring the hardest. His big white fluffy body was shaking so hard that he shook loose a few wisps of down.

"Really! Boron! It's not a laughing matter," his mate said in dismay.

"But it is, my dear. That's the point." And he began to laugh even harder.

The owls had already settled down for the day. It had been several hours since Madame Plonk had sung her lovely "Night Is Done" song and all had wished one another good light until the next night. But Soren had trouble falling asleep, and then he woke up in that slow time of the day for owls, when silence seems to press down over everything and the air is thick with sunlight and the minutes drag by. Time seemed to crawl and one wondered if there would ever be blackness again. Once more Soren felt that melancholy feeling. He was not sure exactly what was causing it. He should be so happy here. He did feel bad about their misbehaviour at tea. Good manners meant a lot to Mrs P. He hated disappointing her. *Maybe,* he thought, *I should go and apologise.* Mrs Plithiver was often up at this time of the day. Perhaps he would make his way down to her hollow. She lived there with two other nest-maids.

The three snakes shared a mossy pocket in the tree nearly one hundred feet below where Soren slept. It smelled of damp shredded bark, moss, and warm stones. The nest-maid snakes enjoyed sleeping with warm stones, so these stones were part of the furnishings of any hollow in which they slept. Bubo always heated up several so they could have them in their quarters. Soren rather liked the smell. The heat from the stones released the fragrance of the moss, and the moss that grew on the Great Ga'Hoole Tree was especially sweet. It was used in a soup that was made by Cook. There was barely a part of the Great Ga'Hoole Tree that was not used for something. It was for this reason that the owls so carefully nurtured and cared for their home – never overpicking the milkberries, and burying their pellets around the roots of the tree where their rich, nourishing contents would be most directly absorbed.

The fragrance of the moss and warm stones drifted up to Soren as he made his way down. He stopped at the opening of the pocket and peered in. But before he could even speak, Mrs P must have sensed his presence.

"Soren, dear boy, what are you doing up this time of day? Come on in, young one."

"Aren't the other nest-maids asleep?"

"Oh, no. They're all out doing guild business."

There were several guilds: the harp guild, the lacemakers', weavers', and others to which the nest snakes belonged. One had to be chosen. It was rather like the tapping ceremony for the chaws. Mrs Plithiver had not been chosen yet for any guild.

"Mrs P, I came to apologise for my disgusting behaviour at tea. I am truly sorry. I know that..."

Mrs P coiled up and cocked her head in that particularly sympathetic way she had. "Soren," she spoke softly and there was something in the very softness of her voice that brought tears to his eyes. "Soren, dear boy, I know you are sorry, but I don't think that is why you are here."

"It's not?" Soren was dumbfounded. But she was right. That really wasn't why he was here. He knew it as soon as she had said it. Yet he was still confused. "Why... why," he stammered, "am I here?"

"I think it has to do with your sister Eglantine."

As soon as she said it, Soren knew that she was right. He missed his parents terribly but he did not worry about his parents. Eglantine, however, was another story. Mrs P had her suspicions about Kludd. These suspicions deepened when Kludd threatened to eat her. Still, she was not sure if Eglantine had been snatched or not. Eglantine had simply disappeared.

"It's the not knowing, isn't it, that's so hard. Not knowing if Eglantine is dead or alive..."

"Or imprisoned," Soren said.

"Yes, dear. I know."

"And if she is dead, it doesn't help me one bit to think of her being in glaumora if I am here and she is there."

"No, of course not. She's too young to be in glaumora."

"Mrs P, I know that St Aegolius Academy for Orphan Owls is the most terrible place. But remember what the dying Barred Owl said about," Soren dropped his voice, "the 'you only wish'…"

"Hush now, dear."

Soren simply couldn't stop himself. "Have you heard anything else about the 'you only wish'?"

Mrs Plithiver waved her head about in a small figure eight, which was the manner in which blind snakes often moved when they could not quite decide what to say or do. Soren peered at her closely. Was something leaking out of the small dents where her eyes would have been? Soren suddenly felt terrible. "I'm sorry, Mrs P. I won't speak of this again."

"No, dear. Come to me whenever you want to talk about Eglantine. I think it will help you, but let's not get carried away with rumours of terrible places. I have a feeling deep within me that Eglantine is not dead. Now, I cannot tell you more than that, but I think together we can hope. Hope is never a foolish thing – although others will tell you it is. But I don't need to tell you that, Soren – look at yourself. You were snatched and you taught yourself to fly and you escaped from that awful St Aggie's. You flew straight out of those deep stone canyons and right into the Yonder. Anyone who flies out of a stone hole into the Yonder knows about hope."

It was always this way when Soren spoke with Mrs P. She always made him feel so much better. It was just as if a clean rain had washed away all of the worry and the sadness. Yes, he still missed his parents. He would always miss his parents, and he would never get used to it, but Mrs P had given him hope about Eglantine, and this alone made him feel so much better. He decided to take the outside route back to his hollow. The day guard on this side of the tree was very nice and wouldn't mind that he had gone down to see his old nest-maid. And there weren't any real rules at the Great Ga'Hoole Tree about having to stay in your hollow asleep all day until the wake-up calls of good night. So he stepped out on a branch and lifted into flight, swooping through the spreading limbs of the old tree. Yes, Mrs P was right. He could see the beginnings of the new milkberries forming on the long glistening threads they called silver rain at this time of the year.

These slim vines cascaded down from branches of the Great Ga'Hoole Tree and swayed like sheer curtains in the afternoon sun. In winter they were white and then in spring they turned silvery, by summer they would be golden, and by autumn they would turn a deep coppery rose. Thus, in Ga'Hoole the seasons were not simply called winter, summer, spring and autumn, but the times of the white rain, the silver rain, the golden rain and the rain of the copper rose. For the young owls, there was nothing more fun than to fly amid the glistening curtains. Therefore they had developed all sorts of games to be played. But on this bright afternoon, everyone was asleep so Soren found himself alone. Rain must have just fallen, for the vines sparkled with beads of water and behind one curtain he caught the shimmering colours of a rainbow.

"Lovely, isn't it?" A voice melted like a chime out of the silver rain. It was Madame Plonk, the harp singer, who sang them to sleep every morning. She was a Snowy Owl and as she sailed through the silver rain Soren blinked in amazement, for he had never seen such a beautiful sight. She was no longer snowy white but indeed had become a living, flying rainbow. All colours seemed to radiate from her plumage.

Soren wished that one of the chaws of the Great Ga'Hoole Tree could be learning the harp and singing from Madame Plonk. But the pluckers of the harp were never owls, only blind snakes. And the only ones trained to sing were direct descendants of the Plonk line of Snowy Owls.

They flew, weaving themselves through the vines and the hues of the rainbow for a few more minutes. Then Madame Plonk said, "Time for me to go, dear. Wake-up time. Evensong must be sung. I see the snakes coming out now, making their way towards the harp. Can't be late. But I've so enjoyed our afternoon flight. We'll do it again sometime. Or drop by for a cup of milkberry tea."

Soren wondered if he would ever have the nerve to just 'drop by' Madame Plonk's for a cup of tea. What would he ever have to say to such a beautiful and elegant owl? Flying was one thing, but sitting and talking was another. Soren saw dozens of rosy-scaled blind snakes crawling up to the hollow where the harp was kept. Soon the Great Ga'Hoole Tree would begin to awake and stir to the lovely harmonies of Evensong. For twilight was upon them.

CHAPTER THIRTEEN

Books of the Yonder

"Now, young ones, please follow me as we explore the wondrous root structure of our dear tree. You see where the roots bump up from the ground." It was the Ga'Hoolology ryb, a boring old Burrowing Owl.

"Here's one."

"Oh, yes, Otulissa. A perfect example."

"Here's one," Gylfie mimicked Otulissa. "She has the most annoying voice."

"Now if we can find a pellet or if someone would care to yarp one, I shall demonstrate the proper burying technique. Pellets properly buried nourish the tree," the ryb continued.

"Oh, I'll find you one," Otulissa quickly volunteered and bustled off.

"This is the most borrring class," sighed Soren. They had been stomping around the base of the Great Ga'Hoole Tree all during twilight.

"I don't think it's that bad," said Digger. Digger of course, being a Burrowing Owl, preferred ground activities.

"I don't know what I'll do if I am tapped for Ga'Hoolology," Twilight muttered.

"You? Never," Soren said, but he was secretly worried that he might be. He realised that knowing about the tree was important. The Ga'Hoolology ryb constantly drummed this into them just as she was doing now. "The Great Ga'Hoole Tree has thrived and flourished for these thousands of years because the owls have been such excellent stewards of this little piece of earth that the Great Glaux gave them." Twilight began to mouth the words as she said them.

"That is so rude," Otulissa hissed.

"Oh, go yarp a pellet!" Twilight barked back.

"What's that? Someone has a pellet to yarp? Twilight dear, come up here. I believe I heard you say you had a little gift to bestow on our Great Ga'Hoole Tree."

*   *   *

133

Class finally ended an hour before First Black. There was still time to go to the library. This was Soren and Gylfie's favourite place in the old tree. The two young owls had a special fondness for libraries that went beyond the wonderful books that they were now learning how to read. At St Aegolius Academy, the library had been strictly off-limits to everyone except for Skench and Spoorn, the two brutal owls who ran the orphanage. No one knew how to read at St Aggie's except for Skench and Spoorn, but here everyone knew how to read and they read constantly. But the reason why libraries were so special to Gylfie and Soren was that it was from the library at St Aggie's that they had escaped.

For the two young owls libraries meant freedom in every way. Sometimes Soren thought that libraries for him were a kind of Yonder, in the sense that Mrs Plithiver and other snakes spoke of the sky. The sky so far away for snakes, as far as anything could be, was a world unseen. But as Soren and Gylfie learned to read they began to get glimmerings of worlds unseen.

The only problem with the library was the old Whiskered Screech, Ezylryb. He was always there, and he was still as frightening as he had been that day when Soren first saw him in the parliament and felt his squinted eye burning into him. The old bird rarely spoke and when he did it was in a low, growlish hoot. He had a fondness for caterpillars and kept a store of dried ones for when they were out of season. These he put in a little pile by his desk in the library. It was not what Ezylryb said that Soren and Gylfie found unnerving, it was what he didn't say. He seemed to quietly observe everything even as he read with his one and a half eyes. Every once in a while he emitted a low growl of what they could only feel was disapproval. But worst of all was his deformed foot. And although Soren and Gylfie knew it was impolite to stare, their eyes just seemed drawn to that foot. Soren admitted to Gylfie that he couldn't help it, and Gylfie said that she herself was fearful of making a terrible slip.

"Remember when Matron came in the other day to serve tea and she asked me to take the cup to him and to ask if he wanted his usual with it – whatever that was. I was so afraid I was going to say something like, 'Ezylryb, Matron would like to know if you'd like your tea with your usual fourth talon'." Soren laughed but he knew exactly what Gylfie meant.

There were, however, too many compelling reasons to go to the library. So they went and learned to ignore his occasional growlish hoots, trying not to stare at his foot and trying to avoid the amber squint of his eye. The library was quite high in the great tree in a roomy hollow that was lined with books, and the floor was spread with lovely carpets woven of mosses, grasses and occasional strands of down. When Soren and Gylfie entered, they spotted Ezylryb in his usual spot. There was the pile of caterpillars. Every now and then he would pluck one and munch it. His beak was now poked into a book entitled *Magnetic Properties as They Occur Naturally and Unnaturally in Nature.*

Soren made his way towards a shelf that had books about barns and churches for, once upon a time Barn Owls like himself had actually lived in such places and Soren enjoyed looking at the pictures and reading about them. Some of the churches were magnificent, with windows stained the colours of rainbows and stone spires that soared high into the sky. But Soren actually preferred the simpler little wooden churches, neatly painted, with something called steeples for their bells. Gylfie liked books with poems, funny riddles, and jokes. She went to see if a book she had discovered yesterday was still there, called *Hooties, Cooties and Nooties: A Book of Owl Humour with Recipes, Jokes and Practical Advice.* It was written by Philomena Bagwhistle, a well-known nest-maid snake who had spent many years in service.

But just as Gylfie was about to pull the book from the shelf there was a low growl. "You can do better than that, young one. One day with that Philomena Bagwhistle slop is quite 'nuff, I'd say. Whyn't try something a little weightier?"

"Like what?" Gylfie said in a small voice.

"Try that one over there." Ezylryb raised his foot, the one with three talons, and pointed.

Soren froze. He could not take his eyes off the talons. Was it a deformity that he had been born with, as some said, or had it been snapped off in a mobbing by crows? The three talons raked the air as he pointed, and Soren and Gylfie's feathers automatically drooped as owl feathers do when they find themselves in conditions of fear. The old owl now got up from his desk, lurched towards the shelf and pulled the book off using only one talon. Gylfie's and Soren's eyes were riveted on the talon. "Look at the book, idiots, not my talons. Or here, take a good look at the talons so you can get used to it." And he shook the deformed foot in their faces. The two owls nearly fainted on the spot.

"We're used to it," Soren gasped.

"Good. Now read the book," Ezylryb said.

Gylfie began sounding out the words, *"Tempers of the Gizzard: An Interpretative Physiology of This Vital Organ in Strigiformes."*

"What are Strigiformes?" whispered Soren.

"Us," Gylfie said softly. "That's the fancy name for all owls, whether we're Elf Owls or Barn Owls or…" Gylfie hesitated, "a Whiskered Screech."

"Right-o. Now go on, the both of you. Try something harder. Read it together." He fixed them in his amber squint. "And you can now quit wasting time thinking about my three talons. If you want to see it again you can." He gave a little wave, and then with his odd gait made his way back to his desk, stopping on the way to poke the small fire in the grate.

Soren and Gylfie opened the book. Thank goodness there were lots of pictures but they had a go at the first paragraph.

The gizzard is a most marvellous organ. Considered the second stomach in owls and often called the muscular stomach, it filters out indigestible items such as bone, fur, hair, feathers, and teeth. The gizzard compresses the indigestible parts into a pellet. The pellets are yarped through the beak. [See footnote pertaining to identification of owl species through pellet analysis.]

"I think we can skip the footnotes," Soren whispered, hoping that Ezylryb wouldn't hear. "This is boring enough as it is."

"Oh, I always skip the footnotes," Gylfie said.

"How many books with footnotes have you read, Gylfie?" Soren blinked in surprise.

"One. It was about feather maintenance. But look." Gylfie pointed with her talon to the next paragraph.

Volumes have been written about the physical processes of the gizzard. But rarely do we find much in the literature concerning the temper of this marvellous organ. This seems like a gross oversight. For do we not attribute all of our most profound feelings to the sensitivity of this muscular organ? How many times a day does an owl think, "Oh, I feel it in my gizzard?" When we feel a strong passion, or perhaps trust, or even distrust, this is our first reaction.

"Well, that's the truth," Soren said. "There's not much new in that. Hardly original."

"Hold on, Soren. Look what he says here."

We do use our gizzards as our guide. Our gizzards, indeed, do often navigate us over treacherous emotional terrain. However, it is my considered opinion that the immature owl does not always know for certain his gizzardly instincts. Why do so many break the one rule their parents tell them never to break and try to fly too young, thus falling out of nests? Stubbornness. They have blocked out certain subtle signals their gizzards might be sending them...

Soren looked up and saw Ezylryb staring at them. "Why do you suppose he's having us read this, Gylfie?"

"I think he's trying to send us a message," Gylfie replied.

"What? *Don't be stubborn? Open up your gizzard?*"

"I don't know, but it's almost time for night flight exercises."

They closed the book and then backed out of the library, making short little bobbing gestures to Ezylryb. "Very interesting," Gylfie said. "Thank you for the suggestion."

"Yes, thank you," Soren said.

Ezylryb said nothing. He only coughed a ragged hoot and plucked another caterpillar from the pile.

"Great Glaux, I'll just die if I get tapped for the weather interpretation chaw. I mean, can you imagine having Ezylryb as your chaw leader? It's just too creepy to even think about," Soren said.

"You know if you get tapped for colliering, you automatically have to take weather interpretation and fly with that chaw as well," Gylfie said.

"Well, who wants to get tapped for colliering and get their beak singed anyway?" Soren replied dejectedly.

"You didn't get it singed when you picked up the coal that you dropped on that bobcat."

"We were all picking them up when we were burying them."

"Yeah, but you flew with yours!"

"That was pure dumb luck."

"Maybe, but if you do it properly you never get singed, and that's what Bubo helps teach. It would be great to have Bubo as a chaw leader."

"Yeah, but if you get Ezylryb with him I would hardly call that a bargain. I think Bubo only helps. It's that other old owl, Elvan, who is the leader of colliering. I still don't see why you have to do weather with colliering."

"Well, you have to fly into forest fires and pick up burning embers. And forest fires, they say, are like a weather system all by themselves. You have to know about the drafts and winds that the heat can cause. I heard Bubo talking about it the other day."

Soren decided not to worry about it.

Just at that moment Digger came up. "Ready for night flight, Digger?" Soren asked.

"Yes. And I've really improved. Much stronger, that's what Boron says. Wait until you see me."

CHAPTER FOURTEEN

Night flight

The night flight was always fun. There was never any special purpose to it. It really was mostly recreational. Boron liked to get all the newly arrived owls together with some of the other young owls in the blackness of the sky so they could, as he put it, "Buddy up, tell a few jokes, yarp a few pellets, and hoot at the moon."

"So, Twilight," Boron began. "I've got one that you'll like. Did you hear the story of the wet pooper who was flying over Hoolemere and hit a fish?"

Otulissa dropped back to where Soren was flying. "He's just too much," she muttered.

"Who's too much?" Soren asked.

"Our king, Boron. He's telling a wet poop joke. I think it's undignified for one of his position."

Soren sighed. "Give it a blow, Otulissa." This was not the most polite way for an owl to say, "A little less serious, please".

"Well, I sure hope he doesn't head a chaw. I would find it most unpleasant. You know, tonight the tappings begin."

"They do?"

"Yes, and I just have a feeling in my gizzard that I'm going to find ten nuts in my bedding down."

Each chaw had symbolic objects that the leader left in a young owl's bedding. Find ten nuts arranged in the pattern of the Great Glaux constellation when you went to sleep at First Light, and that meant you were in the navigation chaw of Strix Struma. A pellet was for the tracking chaw, a milkberry for the Ga'Hoology chaw. A molted feather was the symbol for the search-and-rescue chaw. A dried caterpillar was naturally for Ezylryb's weather chaw. A piece of coal and a caterpillar meant that you had been picked for colliering and were by necessity in for double duty and required to fly with the weather chaw as well.

"Don't you have any feelings, Soren?" Otulissa asked.

"I prefer not to discuss my gizzardly feelings," he replied almost primly.

"Why not?"

"I don't know. I'm just not comfortable doing it. You know I don't mean to be rude, Otulissa, but for someone so well bred you push awfully hard."

"Well, honestly." Otulissa turned to Primrose, who was flying rather noisily due to her lack of plummels, the fringes at the edge of the flight feathers that helped owls fly in silence. Neither Pygmy nor Elf owls had such fringes. "What about you, Primrose? Any little twinges in the old gizzard?"

"Oh, I don't know, Otulissa. One minute I think I'm a sure bet for search-and-rescue, which I'd love, and then the next, I think they'll tap me for tracking, which I guess I wouldn't mind. You know, I just don't know. I mean, I think that's part of the problem."

"What do you mean – what problem?"

"My gizzard – it's just so here, there, everywhere. I mean, when you said 'old gizzard', I realised my gizzard isn't so old, nor is yours for that matter, but you seem to know it better."

"Oh, I know my gizzard." Otulissa nodded smugly.

"Lucky you," Primrose sighed.

Soren had been listening and blinked in wonderment at Primrose's words. They were exactly what the author of the book had been talking about – the immature gizzard of an immature owl.

Soren cut behind Otulissa and came up on the windward side of Primrose. "Primrose, were you in the library reading that book about the physiology and the temper of owl gizzards?"

"Oh, great Glaux, no. I only read joke books and romances for the most part, and never anything with any 'ology' in the title. Do you know that Madame Plonk has written a memoir about her love life? She's had a lot of mates who died. The book is called *My Fabulous Life and Times: An Anecdotal History of a Life Devoted to Love and Song.* There's a lot about music in it. I love Madame Plonk."

"Who wants to read about that?" Twilight flew up. "Enough to make a person yarp, all that romantic stuff. I like reading about weapons, battle claws, war hammers."

"Well," said Otulissa, "I don't especially like reading about weapons but I find Madame Plonk coarse and unrefined, and they say she's got a touch of the magpie in her. Have you ever been to her 'apartments', as she calls them?"

"Oh, yes," Primrose made a rapturous little low hooting noise. "Aren't they beautiful?"

"Oh, yes, beautiful with other creatures' things –

bits of crockery and teacups made out of something she calls porcelain. Now where would she get that stuff? Well, I think under all those snowy white feathers is a magpie in disguise – that's what I think. And frankly, I find the apartment vulgar – rather like its occupant."

Great Glaux, she's obnoxious, Soren thought. Simply to change the subject, Soren decided to ask Otulissa how she came to the Great Ga'Hoole Tree.

"When did you come here, Otulissa?"

"It was during the time of the copper rose rain. I came from Ambala. You might have heard that Ambala suffered a great many egg snatchings because of St Aggie's patrols. My mother and father had lost two eggs this way and had gone out to see if they could find them somehow. I was left in the nest under the care of a very distracted aunt of mine. Well, she decided to go visit a friend, and I became worried. I couldn't fly yet, and don't for a minute think I was trying to. I was a very obedient owlet. I was only looking over the edge for Auntie, and I just fell. It's the honest truth."

Racdrops it is, Soren thought. She was doing what many other owlets had tried to do, like Gylfie and dozens of others, trying to fly. Except Gylfie had admitted it. Otulissa wasn't all that different. If she just wasn't so smug about everything.

"Luckily," Otulissa continued, "some search-and-rescue patrols from the Great Ga'Hoole Tree came by and found me. They put me back into my nest and we waited and waited for my aunt and for my parents, but none of them ever returned. So I must assume that they met with disaster trying to recover the eggs. Of course, my aunt, well, I'm not sure what really happened to her. As I said, she was a very scatterbrained owl – for a Spotted one. In any case, the patrols took me back here to the Great Ga'Hoole Tree." She paused for a second, then blinked. "I'm an orphan like you."

Soren was taken aback. It was perhaps the nicest thing that Otulissa had ever said. Otulissa seldom thought of herself being like anyone else or sharing any traits, except with the most elegant and distinguished of her Strix ancestors.

Boron had just clacked his beak loudly, announcing that night flight was finished and he had spotted Strix Struma making her way upwind to take over for navigation class.

"It will be a short class tonight, young ones," she announced upon arriving. "For as you know, this is a special night and we want to be sure to get back before First Light."

*　　*　　*

So indeed they returned to the Great Ga'Hoole Tree at that border of darkness that owls call the Deep Grey, when the black has faded but the sun has not yet spilled even the first sliver of a ray over the horizon. Nobody really wanted tea. It all took too long and the nest snakes seemed unbearably slow as they slithered in with the cups on their backs. It was an unusually silent teatime. It was as if everyone was too worried to speak, and there was absolutely no talk about feelings in one's gizzard. Even Otulissa had shut up.

"No seconds, anyone?" Mrs P said. "I'd be happy to go back and get some, and there are more nice little nut cakes."

Soren saw Otulissa blink her eyes shut for the longest time. He knew exactly what she was thinking about: nuts, and not the ones that had been baked in a cake. No, she was thinking of ten nuts arranged in the figure of the Great Glaux constellation. He almost felt sorry for her.

Finally, the time came for good light. Madame Plonk would, of course, sing the beautiful good light song, and then they were allowed to look into the down fluff and discover their destinies. Usually, after Madame Plonk's song there was total silence, but there would not be tonight. Instead, there would be raucous shrieks mixed with some groans, and owls saying, "I told you so. I knew you'd get into that chaw". While others would be quietly thinking, *How shall I survive Ga'Hoolology with that old bore of a Burrowing Owl?*

Soren, Digger, Twilight and Gylfie went to their hollow.

"Well, good luck, everybody," Digger said. "Twilight, I really hope you get what you want. I know how much it means to you."

Suddenly, Soren realised that was his problem. He didn't know what he wanted. He only knew what he didn't want. He truly was an immature owl with an immature gizzard.

They each tucked into their corners. The first chords from the great harp were plucked and then came the soft plings of Madame Plonk's eerily beautiful voice. All too quickly, the last verses of the song came up. Soren felt his heart quicken and a stirring in his gizzard.

Far away is First Black,
But it shall seep back
Over field
Over flower
In the twilight hour.
We are home in our tree.

We are owls, we are free.
As we go, this we know
Glaux is nigh.

Then there were the sounds of owls burrowing into the downy fluff of their beds and then the first gasps. "A pellet!" Digger exclaimed. "I got tracking chaw. I can't believe it!"

Next, a whoop from Twilight. "Hooray! I'm search-and-rescue."

From other hollows came more cries:

"This iron tree is beautiful – great Glaux, I did get metals!"

"A milkberry – oh, no!"

"Ten nuts!!!!" But the voice was not Otulissa's. It was Gylfie's. "Soren, I can't believe it. I didn't think Strix Struma liked me that much," Gylfie whispered as if she couldn't believe her great luck. And then there was silence as six pairs of yellow eyes turned to Soren. "Soren," Digger said, "what did you get?"

"I... I... I'm not sure."

"Not sure?" Gylfie said. They were all puzzled. How could one not be sure?

"I haven't looked yet. I'm scared."

"Soren," Twilight said, "just look. Get it over with. Come on. It can't be so bad."

Can't be so bad? Soren thought. *No, of course, not for all of you who got exactly what you wanted.*

"Come on, Soren," Gylfie said in a softer voice. She had walked over to the pile of down where Soren slept. "Come on. I'll stand right here beside you." Gylfie was half Soren's size but she stretched up and began preening Soren's feathers in a soothing gesture.

Soren sighed and carefully, with one talon, plucked away the down fluff so as not to disturb anything. A dark lump poked through and beside it the shrivelled body of a dried caterpillar.

"Colliering!" the wail peeled out into the morning. But the voice was not that of Soren, who simply stared in disbelief at the piece of coal and the caterpillar. "I can't believe it. I'm on colliering and weather chaws. Disaster!" The voice was that of Otulissa. Great Glaux, Soren thought. As if things weren't bad enough – he was now double chawed with Otulissa!

CHAPTER FIFTEEN

A Visit to Bubo

"One – two – one – two. That's it, Ruby. Tuck the beak…
one – two – one – two…" This was their second chaw
practice for colliering and Soren had never been more
depressed, not since his horrible time at St Aggie's.
The colliering ryb, a Great Grey named Elvan, stood in
the centre of a circle that had been inscribed on the
ground at the base of the tree. It was near the forge
where Bubo worked, keeping them supplied with red-
hot coals. Elvan barked commands at them and
insisted that they march in time as he kept count.
Soren had a deep aversion to marching. They had been
forced to march all the time at St Aggie's. Elvan said
this marching was necessary to establish the proper

rhythm that helped in holding a live coal in their beaks. And it seemed as if his previous experience with live coals in the woods of The Beaks had deserted him. He could hardly believe that he had actually picked up live coals, buried them and flown with them! Soren had spent the first minutes of class being scared and the remainder being bored. If anyone had told him that it was possible to be both in the same practice, he would have said they were yoicks. It was odd that he hardly felt the heat. He remembered thinking this before when he was in the woods of The Beaks. He did notice, however, that Elvan's fringe of light feathers below his beak seemed to be a permanently sooty gray.

Soren thought of his own face, covered in pure white feathers. This was the most distinctive feature of Barn Owls, and he really did not want to think of it growing singed and sooty. Maybe he was vain but he couldn't help it.

"Pay attention! Soren!" Elvan barked. "You nearly ran into Otulissa."

Thank Glaux she can't speak, thought Soren. That was the only good thing about colliering. It was hard to speak with a live coal in one's mouth. So Otulissa was effectively shut up for once.

"All right, rest time. Drop your coals," Elvan announced.

Rest wasn't really rest, however, as the ryb lectured them the entire time. "Tomorrow you shall begin flying with the coals in your beaks. It is not that different, really, from walking. Although you must take care to keep your coal alive and burning."

"Yeah!" Bubo boomed. "Dead coals ain't going to do me a bit of good, young'uns. No sense flying in here with a great lot of ashes, cold as Glaux knows what."

"Yes," continued Elvan. "We don't want to disappoint Bubo."

"Oh, Glaux forbid that we should disappoint Bubo," Otulissa mumbled.

Soren stole a glance at her. There was pure venom in her eyes. Why couldn't she just be angry about being in this chaw? What did Bubo have to do with it? Soren thought. He knew why, of course. Otulissa thought she was too good to have anything to do with Bubo. Neither Bubo nor any of the owls in this chaw had the distinguished background of Otulissa. It was an outrage, as she told Soren forty times a night, that she had not been included in Strix Struma's navigation chaw.

Elvan continued speaking during their break. "And then, of course, after you have had enough nights of weather training we shall find a nice forest fire for you – nothing too big, mind you. Just a nice little beginning fire with a good mix of trees – Ga'Hooles, firs, pine, some soft and hard woods. Not too many ridges or mountains to complicate wind patterns."

"Pardon me," piped up the little Northern Saw-whet Owl, Martin, who had been rescued the same night as Primrose.

"Yes, Martin," Elvan said.

"Well, I don't understand why we need new coals all the time. Once you start a fire going, wouldn't there always be new coals?"

This was some smart little owl, Soren thought. *Why hadn't the others thought of this question? Why were new coals from a new fire needed?*

Elvan turned to Bubo. "Bubo, as chief smith, would you care to answer that?"

"Sure thing, mate." Then he stepped up to Martin and, towering over him, began to speak. "A very good question. You are right, it is very possible to keep fires going forever and that is fine for some things – things like cooking and warming up a hollow. But for certain tasks, especially certain metalwork in the forge, we need new fresh coals that have been born of sparking trees full of sap. They become the blood of our hottest fires. Then again, we need a variety of coals. Certain coals from certain trees last longer. That's how a fire gets bonk."

"But you fly low and slow; that's good for tracking."

"But I've never flown through a forest fire. And I can't wait until weather interpretation – a hurricane! Just imagine flying through that. Life in that ground nest was boring. We were out there in the grasslands – every day just the same. The sound of the wind in the grass just the same, the way the grass moved just the same. Oh yes. Sometimes it moved slower or faster, depending on the wind. But there was a terrible sameness. I can't believe how lucky I am to be double chawed." Ruby sighed with pleasure.

Soren blinked. He wished he felt this way. He wanted to ask Ruby if she was nervous about Ezylryb, but at the same time he didn't want to admit that he was. Ruby was a very tough little owl. She had been brought in by search-and-rescue shortly after Soren had arrived. She had not fallen from a nest, for indeed to fall out of a ground nest was virtually impossible. But something had scared her so badly when her parents were out hunting, she had actually flown before her primaries were fledged. No one was quite sure what had scared her. She had been found exhausted but perched in one of the few trees in the grasslands, declaring, "They'll never find me here! They'll never believe that an immature Short-eared made it to here!" But no one knew who *they* were. And Ruby never said.

Finally, chaw practice was over. Soren dreaded teatime. If it was like yesterday, Twilight would be bragging about his power dives and reverse spiral twists. Gylfie and Digger would both be talking about how exciting their practices were, and he, Soren, would have nothing to say. Maybe he would skip tea. Just as he was having this thought, Bubo waddled over to him.

"It gets better, Soren. It really does. I know this is tough for you. It wasn't the chaw that you wanted, but it's really an honour – double chawed and all. I think you're the first Barn Owl ever to be. Come on now, lad. Come with me. Take tea in the forge. I got some fresh moles, you can have them raw or smoked – whatever takes your fancy, and Cook made a nice milkberry tart."

So Soren followed Bubo into a cave not far from the Great Ga'Hoole Tree, which served as both Bubo's forge and home. Soren had never been in Bubo's cave before and, once one went deep enough into the cave to escape the heat, it was quite comfortable – all fitted up with moleskin rugs and a surprising number of books. Soren had never taken Bubo for a bookish sort of owl.

He could not help but think of the dying Barred Owl's cave and wondered if that owl had been a blacksmith. But a blacksmith for what? That owl had lived completely alone in those woods. Somehow Soren didn't feel comfortable talking to Bubo about the Barred Owl because it made him think of 'you only wish'.

"What's this?" Soren said as he spotted a contraption dangling from the ceiling of the cave. It had bright-coloured things swirling about, catching the reflections of the many lit candles. As the bright bits swirled, they cast spots of colour all over the cave.

"Ah, me whirlyglass. Plonk helped put it together for me."

"Madame Plonk?" Soren couldn't keep the surprise out of his voice. He had never heard anyone refer to her as simply "Plonk".

"Oh, yeah, Plonk and me go back – way back." He winked his eye. Soren wondered if Bubo was part of Madame Plonk's book about her life and fabulous times. "She's got a special relationship with Mags so she can get me lots of bits of glass." Bubo shoved a cup of milkberry tea over to Soren and a morsel of mole. "You know, when you start flying weather with Ezylryb, he won't let you eat meat cooked. He likes you to eat it raw with the fur on it. Says you can't fly into a blizzard or a hurricane with burnt-up meat in your gut and nothing for your gizzard to grind."

"Oh," said Soren. "But who's Mags?"

"Oh dear me, ain't you never heard of Trader Mags?" Soren shook his head. "I forget, you only just got here a bit ago didn't you, and Mags, I guess she hasn't been here since summer."

Bubo pointed a talon at the whirlyglass. "Those bright pieces came from what was called a window in something called a church."

"Churches!" Soren exclaimed. "I know about them. And that's stained glass from their windows! Barn Owls used to live in churches."

"Certainly did. Some still do, live in churches and barns as well, and even castles."

"Castles – what's a castle?"

"Well, it ain't a church and it ain't a barn, but it's a big old fancy thing made from big stones, towers, walls, one of them things that the Others made."

Soren had heard of the Others but he was never exactly sure what the Others were, except that they definitely were not owls, or birds, or really any other living thing that he had ever seen. And, for that matter, they were no longer living. They were creatures from long, long ago, maybe in the time of the first Glaux. Glaux was the most ancient order of owls from which all other owls descended.

"Castles," Soren said dreamily. "Sounds exciting, beautiful – very grand."

"Oh, grand indeed. But you ask me, no owl, Barn Owl or not, belongs in a church or a barn or a castle. Better life in a tree."

"But you live in a cave."

"That's different."

"I don't see why."

Bubo squinted one eye at Soren as if studying him more closely. "Got a lively mind, don't you, lad?"

"I don't know." Soren shrugged self-consciously.

Then, as if trying to change the direction of the conversation, Bubo said abruptly, "Don't you want to know about glass?" Soren nodded again. "Well," continued Bubo, "the churches and castles, they have these windows made of glass and they coloured the glass."

"Oh, I read about that in a book in the library."

"Yes, they made it all pretty. Well, Mags the trader, she knows where there are a lot of broken-down old churches with smashed-up windows. Leave it to a magpie to find such bits, but that's their nature and she knows Plonkie."

Plonkie! Soren thought, *They must have been close!*

"Plonkie has a weakness for all these coloured bits and things. So Mags always brings a bagful with her here when she comes to trade. Plonk thought this place needed brightening up" – Bubo gestured around the cave with his talons – "so she made me this whirlyglass. Plonk has a number of them in her apartments – as she call her place – ridiculous name, if you ask me."

It did brighten it up, but Soren couldn't help but ask another question. "Don't you miss living in a tree? I mean, it's not like you were born a Burrowing Owl used to living in holes. Don't you miss the sky?"

Soren thought of his own hollow that he shared with Gylfie and Twilight and Digger. There was an opening just the shape of an owl's beak through which they could glimpse the sky. So during the day there was always a pretty slice of blue in their hollow and when they came back from night flights before the dawn rose, it perfectly framed the last of the evening stars. They could feel the wind and hear the stirring of the milkberry vines. Soren did not think he would like living in a cave.

"I warn't born a Burrowing Owl, that's the truth. I be a Great Horned, and it ain't customary for any

Great Horned to go about life in a cave. But you see, I be a smith. It's in my gizzard, this feeling for the metals." He gestured towards his bookshelf that indeed had many books about metals and forging.

"And we smiths, no matter if we're Great Greys or Great Horneds or Snowies or Spotted Owls, get these special feelings in the old gizzard, you know. We fly, yes, we love the sky, but we is drawn to the earth as well – not like the Burrowing Owls, not the same thing at all. It be a strange and most peculiar force. It's as if all these years working with the iron, we get a bit of the magnet in us, you know. Like them special metals, you know, iron. It's got what we call a field. Well, you'll be learning this in metals class, in higher magnetics, where all the unseeable parts are lined up. It makes this force that draws you – same thing with me – I get drawn to the very earth from which them little flecks of iron come from."

"Flecks!" Soren nearly screamed. Flecks were part of Soren's worst memories from St Aggie's.

"What's a matter, boy? You gotta yarp? Go right ahead. We ain't formal around here."

"At St Aggie's, they made us pick apart pellets for bones and things and then something they called 'flecks'. Only first-degree pickers could pick for flecks."

"You don't say?" Bubo blinked his eyes.

"But Gylfie and I never knew what flecks were. And, of course, we could never ask. But we did know they were kept in the library."

"Odd place to keep iron."

"Is that what flecks are – iron?"

"Yes, in their smallest bits, but better if you can find a nice big hunk of iron ore, just like if you can find a nice hunk of silver or gold in a creek. The metals chaw brought me back a very handsome piece of gold the other day. Wouldn't you know Plonk spotted me with it practically as soon as they lit down and was all over me to make something for her. 'Course Boron and Barran will have a thing or two to say 'bout that. Silver, gold, that is all kept for the whole tree and not for one vain old Snowy with a taste for the glitter." He made the soft churring sound of laughter.

"Speaking of which, Plonk's going to start singing good light any minute. You better fly on up to your hollow. A lot to do tomorrow. Elvan thinks you'll be ready to fly with the coals. Now you pay attention, son. Don't go smacking into Otulissa like you nearly did in practice." Then he squinted at Soren. "You know, not everyone is chosen to be double chawed like you. Boron and Barran must think you got something special. And Ezylryb, too."

"But why me? I don't get it. I'm not that special."

"Oh, but you are. You had the mark on you."

"The mark on me? What are you talking about?"

"Ezylryb spotted it. None of the rest of us could see it, of course. He got something special with that squinted eye of his. You'd been messing about with coals – hadn't you, lad? Ain't nothing to be ashamed of. Good Glaux, no! Flew with one, maybe?" Bubo cocked his head and looked quizzically at Soren.

"I did, but I washed off the smudge."

"Ah, but you still be marked. Only none else can see it, except Ezylryb. He's a tough one, Ezylryb. And smart! Smartest owl in the whole place. He wouldn't just choose any old owl. He wanted you, mark or no mark. So you be all you can be, Soren."

Be all you can be. What exactly did that mean? Especially when he wasn't even sure what he wanted to be, except not in a double chaw with Otulissa and with Ezylryb as his ryb. Soren kept thinking of Bubo's words long after Madame Plonk's song had ended, and Twilight and Gylfie and Digger were asleep. Or at least he thought so. But just then he heard the slightly raspy voice of Digger curling through the milky light that slipped in through the opening of their hollow.

"Soren, are you all right?"

"Yeah, why?"

"I'm just worried about you. I mean, you've been so quiet since the tapping, and you didn't come to tea and all."

"Well, don't worry, Digger, it's not your problem."

"But it is."

"No, it's not, Digger. You worry too much. You just need to worry about yourself. Not me. That's not your job."

"It's not a job, Soren," Digger said with a slight edge in his voice. "It is what I am."

"Now what do you mean by that?"

"Well, you might think I'm only a Burrowing Owl, you know, perfect for tracking with my long strong legs, but I am more than just this bunch of feathers and bare legs. I can't explain it. I just feel things. And right now I am feeling very sorry, very bad for you."

Soren blinked. He thought about what Digger had just said. It made him think of his conversation with Bubo, who had, in a sense, said the same thing. When he asked Bubo why he lived in a cave, he said that he was not simply a Great Horned Owl. In other words, Bubo, like Digger, was not just a bunch of feathers on a pair of legs, weak or strong, with a pair of wings. He was something more, and it was this that had drawn him to a cave in the earth to live, closer to the metals he knew and worked with. Maybe this was what Bubo had meant when he told Soren to be all he could be. Maybe it had something to do with an owl's true nature that went beyond his or her species as a Barn Owl or a Burrowing Owl. Soren's head swirled with these confusing thoughts.

Then Digger asked a truly astounding question. "Soren, what do you think it means to be an owl?"

"I don't know. I mean, I'm not sure what you mean."

"I'm not sure, either," Digger said. "But it's just as if it is so easy to describe us. You know, there are so many things that we have that are different from other birds, but do you really think that is the meaning of being an owl? Just because our heads can spin nearly all the way around, that we can see what other birds cannot at night, that we fly slow and silent – is it just these differences that make us owls?"

"Digger, why do you ask these questions? They're impossible to answer."

"Maybe that's why I ask them – because they are impossible to answer. It's kind of exciting. It means that there can be unexpected truths and meanings to why we are what we are. You see – that is why I know I am much more than strong legs and weak wings.

And you are too, Soren – you are more than your lovely white face and your sharp ears that can hear anything and your strange black eyes."

Digger was a curious owl. There was certainly no doubt about it. Soren looked out the opening into the last of the morning as it began to blare into the lightness of midday. If what Digger said was true – that there were unexpected truths and meanings to be found, Soren wondered what that might mean for him. He looked at his friends sleeping peacefully now: Twilight, huge, a luminous silvery grey in the morning light; Gylfie, like a little dusty smudge not much longer than one of Twilight's talons; and Digger, his peculiar, featherless legs, long and sinewy, his stubby tail and his rather flattish head.

Soren remembered when, in anticipation of going to the Great Ga'Hoole Tree, he and Gylfie imagined it as just the opposite of St Aggie's, but it was really much more. And maybe he could become more too. The beak-shaped opening in the hollow flared white in the noonday sun as Soren finally fell asleep.

CHAPTER SIXTEEN

The Voices in the Roots

"Psst... pssst," something hissed in Soren's ear.

"Gylfie, what are you doing up at this hour? It's broad daylight. Are you yoicks?"

"Not at all." Soren could see that Gylfie was practically hopping up and down with excitement. "Soren, there's a very important meeting going on in the parliament hollow."

"So?"

"Soren, I think they are talking about the Barred Owl and" – Gylfie gulped and shut her eyes tight – "and... and..." Gylfie was seldom at a loss for words. "The 'you only wish'."

Soren was suddenly fully awake. "You're kidding."

"I wouldn't kid about something like this, Soren, and you know it."

"How do you know this? I mean, how did you find out? Were you in the meeting?"

Gylfie blinked and looked down at her tiny talons in embarrassment. "Look, I know it's not nice to eavesdrop, but I couldn't sleep and you know how Cook always says come down to the kitchen if we can't sleep and she'll make us a nice cup of milkberry tea. So I went down, and on my way back I just thought I'd take a different route, so I followed one of those deep inner passageways that is very winding and pretty narrow, and it actually started to go down instead of up towards the sleeping hollows. There's a spot where something happens to the timber of the Great Ga'Hoole Tree. It is very thin and I could hear voices, and then I found this perfect slot that is just Elf Owl size."

"Do they have one just Barn Owl size?" Soren interrupted.

"Maybe. There's an even better one my size higher up, but I would need a perch."

"At your service, Gylf!" Twilight was suddenly awake. "What a team we'll make. On the shoulders of giants, the little Elf will bring back the word!"

"Twilight, puhleeze!" Soren said.

"Why not? Makes perfect sense."

"Well, I might not be a giant like you, but I can hear better than any of you. I'm going too. So count me in," said Soren.

"Me, too." Digger was stretching his legs and seemed at least half awake.

"Do you even know what we're talking about?" Gylfie turned to the Burrowing Owl.

"No, but we're a band, remember? Nobody gets left out. Fill me in on the way to whatever we're doing."

And so the band of four, as quietly as possible, moved out of their hollow with Gylfie in the lead. They left by the sky opening and flew a quarter of the way down the tree, where they entered a very small opening that Gylfie had discovered, which twisted and turned, pitched and curled through the huge trunk of the tree, until they had wound around to the back side of the Parliament hollow and found themselves actually slightly beneath that hollow, in the root structure of the tree. It was not that the walls were thin, Soren soon realised. It was rather that the roots of the Great Ga'Hoole Tree were transmitting the sounds.

Gylfie hopped on Twilight's shoulders and Soren pressed one ear to a root, as did Digger.

"And so you say, Bubo, that no trace of the dear

Barred Owl was found? Our noble servant perished in the region of The Beaks?"

The four eavesdropping owls blinked and suppressed gasps of astonishment. It had to be the same owl. It just had to. Soren pressed his ear closer.

"Not rightly sure if he exactly perished, Boron. I mean he mightn't be dead. He might just be captured."

"By St Aggie's patrols or..." Now all four owls strained to hear, but they could not make out what Boron had said. Indeed, it seemed as if there was a little hole in the conversation, as if a word had dropped out, perhaps a word too awful to say. Soren wasn't sure. But he felt a chill run through him.

"Either way it's a bad piece of work." It was Ezylryb's voice. Soren could tell.

"We done lost one of our best slipgizzles and a darned fine smith as well, one of the best of the rogues." Bubo was speaking again.

What is a slipgizzle? Digger mouthed the words. Soren shrugged. He had never heard the word before. He might have heard the word 'rogue' but he wasn't sure what that meant either.

"Without a reliable slipgizzle," now Barran was speaking, "it's going to make it very difficult to get any information about their activities in The Beaks."

"It was a very strategic spot where he set up his forge."

So that was it! thought Soren. That cave, as Digger had said, not only held the spirit of the Barred Owl within its walls, sooty and scorched by countless fires, but was also his forge. He was a blacksmith, like Bubo. But he was also something else – a slipgizzle. Gradually, the four owls began to understand that a slipgizzle was some sort of owl who listened hard and found out things.

"That old Barred had ears like a Barn Owl," Boron was saying. "We got more information from him than three other slipgizzles put together. And as you said, my dear, his forge in The Beaks was ideally situated near the four points area where Ambala, The Beaks, Kuneer and Tyto almost touch. Couldn't be better. Flew egg guard in Tyto, I hear. Trained up a bunch of young ones to go into Ambala when they were having the worst of their problems... Oh, my. Well, to the immediate business. We must not lose a moment in shoring up the four points region. We're going to need to cultivate a new slipgizzle, of course, but in the meantime we'll have to send out some egg patrols and a small reconnaissance team. Nothing too big. Don't want to attract undue attention. I don't need to tell you how dangerous it will be with the recent reports we've been getting. A lot of groundwork and, as you know, bobcats are numerous there."

"I'll go!" a voice said. Soren blinked. It was that old boring Ga'Hoology ryb.

"Count me in," said Bubo.

"And me." It was the voice of another owl that Soren didn't recognise.

"I think that's enough," Boron spoke in a low voice. "Bubo, you sure about going?"

"'Course I'm sure, sir. He was a smith."

"Yes, Bubo, I know that, but you are our only smith. If we lose you... well, where would we be?"

"I ain't going to get lost, sir. Ain't going to get captured. Ain't going to get eaten by a bobcat. You need me on this mission. I can see what happened in that cave. It takes a smith's eye and a smith's nose to figure something like this out. He couldn't have just vanished into thin air, and I don't believe the Barred could have been captured by St Aggie's or them others. But there'll be clues."

Them others? It was so maddening, Soren thought. Who were they? Who exactly was the "you only wish" Barred Owl?

"Well," continued Boron, "that taken care of, I think the time has now come to honour our brother the Barred Owl, who had no name and elected never to live with us on this island in the middle of the sea, never to be embraced by the lovely ancient limbs of our Great Ga'Hoole Tree, but served as nobly in his own peculiar way as any Knight of Ga'Hoole. Let us raise a flagon of milkberry mead and think gentle thoughts of this brave and noble owl who made safer the hollows and nestlings of so many other owls in the Kingdoms of Ambala, Kuneer and Tyto. Slipgizzle beyond compare, artisan of metals, courageous defender against the growing tides of evil, a Glaux-blessed owl. Hear! Hear!"

And with that, the parliament of owls was adjourned. An immense fluttering swelled up as they left. Soren, Gylfie, Twilight and Digger looked at one another with tears in their eyes.

"And to think," Digger said, "that we are the ones who found him."

"But that's just the problem," said Gylfie. "What do we do now? Tell Boron and Barran?"

"Then they'll know we were eavesdropping," Twilight said.

"Precisely," Gylfie replied.

Soren began to speak slowly, "I think we shouldn't say anything, at least not now. Nothing we will say will change their plans. They still need to send in a reconnaissance team or whatever they call it and find a new slipgizzle. Our knowing that the

Barred Owl is dead and telling them really doesn't change anything."

"I think Soren's right," Gylfie spoke. "You know, eavesdropping like this... well... I have a feeling Boron would really be mad."

"Definitely," said Twilight.

So the four owls wound their way back to their hollow and slept until First Black.

CHAPTER SEVENTEEN

Weather Chaw

A sliver of wet ice hit Soren's face and woke him up abruptly. Outside the hollow, the wind shrieked and a gale raged.

"Great Glaux, it's a mess out there," Twilight muttered.

"It's cold too," said Gylfie, her tiny body shivering.

"Hop under here," Twilight said, and spread one of his enormous wings so that it touched the other side of the hollow and knocked Digger from his bed.

"Twilight!" Digger complained. "Watch it with that wing."

"Gylf is cold."

"I sure hope they will serve something hot for

breakfast," Gylfie said through her clattering beak.

"Me too," said Twilight.

The owls got up and crept from their hollow out on to a madly shaking branch and took off for the dining hollow. There was acorn porridge and steaming cups of milkberry tea, roasted tree slugs and braised mice. But as Soren headed for his place at Mrs Plithiver's, a voice scratched the air.

"Over here, boy. Weather chaw eats it raw with the hair on." It was the unmistakable voice of Ezylryb.

"What?" Soren beaked the word in disbelief.

"You mean you haven't heard?" Otulissa was suddenly beside him.

"Heard what?" Soren said, not sure if he really wanted to know.

"We're having our first weather interpretation chaw tonight."

"You have to be kidding, Otulissa. We aren't going out in this gale."

"Oh, but we are," she said. "And I think it's outrageous. I'm going to have a word with Strix Struma. I'll go right up to Barran if I have to. This is reckless. This is endangering our lives."

"Oh, hush up, dearie. Sit down and eat your mouse – and all the hair, mind you, and that goes for every one of you." It was the fat old blind snake named Octavia, who had served as the weather chaw table for years. Unlike the other blind snakes whose scales were colours varying from rose to pink to a deep coral, Octavia was a pale greenish-blue. Soren sat next to Martin, the smart little Northern Saw-whet who had asked the question in colliering practice about the need for fresh coals. Indeed, Soren realised suddenly that there was more room at the table than he was accustomed to and as he looked about he knew it was because all of the young owls in the weather chaw seemed to have diminished in size. Their feathers were pulled in tightly, indications that the owls were very nervous about their first weather flight. When relaxed, an owl's plumage is loose and fluffy. When angered, owls can puff up their feathers until they appear much, much larger. But now it was as if they had all become suddenly slim. The tension hovered in the air.

Ezylryb fixed the young owls in the amber light of his squinted eye. "Eat up, maties… every single little hair. You've forgotten what raw meat tastes like with the fur, as you call it. Poot here is my first mate. He'll tell you what it's like to fly with no ballast in your gizzard."

"I remember that time before I had acquired the taste for hair and thought I could go through that hurricane. Last time I ever tried that. Nearly got caught in the rim of the eye, I did. Now, you don't want to do that, young'uns." Poot was a Boreal Owl like Soren and Gylfie's old friend Grimble.

"What happens if you get caught in the rim of the eye of a hurricane?" asked Rudy.

"Oh, you spin around till you're dead. Just around and around and around. Awful nasty way to go. Usually get your wings torn off in the process," said Poot.

"Now, don't go scaring them, Poot," Octavia said and gave a ripple so that all their plates clattered a bit. "And please, young'uns, don't try that trick of slipping the fur under the table. Remember, I *am* the table and it itches something fierce."

It was not even dark yet, but the weather chaw owls were already on the take-off limb. It was all they could do to hang on as the gale lashed about them and the limb bucked in the turbulent wind. Shards of ice flew through the air.

"We take off upwind, naturally." Although Soren was not sure in this gale which way upwind even was. "We're going to fly straight out over the Sea of Hoolemere. Try to find the main part of the gale." Ezylryb spoke in short snappish sentences. "Now listen up. Here's what you need to know about a gale, or any storm, really – except for hurricanes – they be a little different with their eyes and all. But what you got in a gale, or storm, is you got your gutter. That's what we call the main trough where the wind runs its punch through. It's at the centre. It not be like the eye in a hurricane. Not nearly so dangerous. Then on either side of the gutter you've got the scuppers. That's where the edge of the winds from the gutters spills over. Then at the very outside edge of the scuppers you got your swillages – more about them later. I fly point. Poot flies what we call upwind scupper. You just follow behind. Do what you're told. Any questions?"

Otulissa raised her talon. "Ezylryb, sir, with all due respect, I have to say that I am surprised that we are going out before it is completely dark. Isn't there a very real danger that in this light we could be mobbed by crows?"

Ezylryb began to laugh and then said, "With all due respect, Otulissa, no one else is yoicks enough to be out on a day like this!"

Soren couldn't help but laugh. But how could he be laughing when he was scared to death? Then again, how could he have been bored in colliering chaw when he was also scared? If this was being all one could be, as Bubo had told him, he certainly had a lot of confusing feelings.

And then suddenly, with an enormous scream, the old Whiskered Screech Owl spread his wings and lifted into the ice-spun twilight.

They flew straight out over the Sea of Hoolemere. The storm was so fierce and the torrents of sleeting rain so thick they could barely see the water, but they did hear the crashing waves. Otulissa was flying near Soren.

"I have never heard of a ryb who used such poor judgment. This is so irresponsible. I am going to have to speak with Boron and Barran. I cannot believe that they would approve of this."

Soren, meanwhile, could not believe that Otulissa could fly through this mess and still keep talking. It took all of his concentration just to fly. The winds seemed to come from every direction. They were constantly buffeted by confused drafts. Martin, the little Saw-whet, was a tumbling blur ahead of him. He had been instructed, as the smallest, to begin flying in Ezylryb's wake for better control.

One minute the owls might be buoyed up several hundred feet and the next they might fly into a dead fall, a kind of hole in the wind, and drop. And of course, there was the ice and rain. Constantly, Soren was having to use the transparent eyelid, the third eyelid that all owls have, to clear out the debris.

Great Glaux, he hoped his third lid didn't simply wear out under these conditions. No wonder Ezylryb squinted. A lifetime of flying into this stuff would be enough to shred any owl's eyelid.

"Oh, for Glaux's sake," Otulissa hissed.

"What now?" Soren said, trying to anticipate the next dead fall, almost hoping for it, to get away from Otulissa.

"He is speaking with seagulls!"

"So?"

"So? How can you say 'so', Soren? I know you come from a very fine family. I can see that you have been well brought up. You must know that seagulls are the absolute worst kind of bird. They are, pardon the coarseness of my language, the scum of the avian world. Trashy, loud. You want nothing to do with them. And look, there he is talking – laughing with them."

"Maybe he's getting weather information from them," Soren said.

"Oh, now that's a thought," Otulissa said and was quiet for several seconds, an amazing occurrence in and of itself. "I think I'll fly up and ask him."

"Don't bother him, Otulissa."

"No, you heard him say if we had any questions we should ask." So off she flew.

"Pardon me, Ezylryb. I am most curious to know why you were – how shall I put it – consorting with seagulls? I thought perhaps it was to gain weather information."

"Seagulls? Oh no, darlin'. They are the dumbest birds on earth and the laziest."

"Well, then why would you even consort with them?"

"I wasn't consorting. I was telling dirty jokes."

"What?" Otulissa gasped.

"Yes, they love wet poop jokes even though they are the wettest of all poopers. 'Oh, tell us another one Ezyl', they always say! And, I must admit, I get a few from them. But the blasted birds are so dumb, half the time they can't remember the punch lines. Very frustrating."

"Well, I never!"

"The jokes were really funny, Otulissa," Martin, the Northern Saw-whet, piped up.

"Now, don't go getting your feathers in a twist, darlin'. You just mind your own business. Get back into position. We're getting near the gutter now. And this is when the fun begins."

"Hoooh-hah!" Poot let out an enormous, raucous hoot. "Here we go, mates. Climbing the baggywrinkles and then straight into the gutter.

Follow us!" The baggywrinkles were the shredded air currents that lay between the scuppers and the gutter. A power thrust was required to get over them. Soren banked and followed the veteran owl, Poot. Martin was in between the two. The tiny owl would get a boost from Poot's speed, as a vacuum would be created, through which he could be sucked up and over the baggywrinkles right into the gutter. Ruby was just ahead of him. She let escape a small joyous hoot. And then suddenly, Soren knew why. Here, at the centre of the gale, in the gutter, the winds all seemed to flow like one great turbulent river. And if one let one's wings sweep slightly forwards, just as Ruby was doing, and angled the tail – well, it was a wonderful sensation, a cross between soaring and gliding – no effort at all. And in the gutter, the ice shards seemed to melt away.

"Oh, tickle me hollow bones. Ain't this the life!" It was Ezylryb, who had dropped back from the point position and now flew between Soren and Otulissa. He yarped a pellet into the river of wind that flowed about them. "Now follow me to the edge of the scuppers, maties, and I'll show you the hurly-burly. And then we'll climb the baggywrinkles and dump right into the scuppers for the ride of your life."

"What is he talking about?" huffed Otulissa. "He should have given us a vocabulary list. He's very disorganised as a teacher."

Why would a vocabulary list matter? Soren thought. What was the use of a word if one could not feel the action in his gizzard? And right now Soren's gizzard was in a fantastic quiver of excitement. This was flying as he had never known it.

"Here we go!" cried Ezylryb. "Now I want to see you punch the wind and then we pop the scuppers and it's tail over talons."

"Oh my heavens!" Otulissa shrieked and Soren gasped as he saw the distinctive three-taloned foot of Ezylryb scratch the moon-smudged sky. He was flying on his back! Then right side up and in the scuppers.

Suddenly, Soren saw a red blur as Ruby did a talons-over-tail somersault and popped the scuppers to join him. "Oh, come on!" she cried. "There's nothing to it."

"Nothing to it. Who's ever heard of an owl flying upside down? I think there's something most unsavoury about it!" Otulissa gasped. "It's reckless, unsafe – yes, unsavoury, unsafe, un-owl."

Oh, shut up! Soren thought and punched the wind just as Ezylryb said, and in a flash he was arcing up towards the sky that spun with dark clouds and was splattered with sheets of icy rain, and then he was right side up in the scuppers next to Ruby.

"Push forwards a bit with your talons and keep angling your tail. It gives you a lot of control and you can ride the waves," Ezylryb called back.

Finally Otulissa arrived, sputtering with rage and talking about a report that she was going to make about "this outrageous activity".

"Oh, shut your beak!" Poot screeched at her. And then they skidded and spun, doing what was called the hurly-burly. In the scuppers, Ezylryb began to squawk a raucous ditty into the teeth of the gale.

We are the owls of the weather chaw.
We take it blistering,
We take it all.
Roiling boiling gusts,
We're the owls with the guts.
For blizzards our gizzards
Do tremble with joy.
An ice storm, a gale, how we love blinding hail.
We fly forwards and backwards,
Upside down and flat.
Do we flinch? Do we wail?
Do we skitter or scutter?
No, we yarp one more pellet

And fly straight for the gutter!
Do we screech? Do we scream?
Do we gurgle? Take pause?
Not on your life!
For we are the best
Of the best of the chaws!

CHAPTER EIGHTEEN

Mrs Plithiver's Dilemma

"Flying upside down!" Primrose gasped. "How do you do that? It's impossible."

"It's not as hard as you think," Soren said excitedly. "It really doesn't take that much skill. It's kind of like when you first start to fly. You have to just sort of believe you can do it."

"But *upside down?*" Gylfie said.

"Do you think a big burly Grey like me could do it?" Twilight said.

"Sure, if the conditions are right. See, that's the problem – you can't try it until you're in the gutter of a gale."

"Gutter of a gale?" Twilight said. "You telling me

a gale has a gutter? Now, I've seen a lot but..." It was hard for Twilight to admit that anyone had seen or experienced something he had not.

Gylfie and Soren looked at each other and blinked in amazement. Twilight did brag, but he did not have that obnoxious sense of superiority that Otulissa had. Still, he was constantly getting reprimanded in his chaw practices for challenging the rybs. Sometimes he could be annoying but, in spite of this, he was a "good soul", as Mrs P would put it. There was never an owl more fiercely loyal than Twilight. As Digger often said, "He makes the best friend and the worst enemy."

"You might not have seen the gutter of a gale," Gylfie said, trying to restrain the peevish note in her voice. "I know you've seen a lot, Twilight, but it is possible that you have not penetrated a gale in the same manner Soren did, under the instruction of Ezylryb."

"Oh, I've flown into the teeth of many a gale, Gylf. I might have been in the gutter and not known I was there. That I admit. Soren here, talking about all this structure of a gale business – just words, you know. No offense, mind you, Soren. But you can fly through something and not know what it's called."

"Yes, I think you're right. Otulissa was making a big fuss about how Ezylryb should have given us a vocabulary list before we took off last night."

"Oh, honestly," Primrose muttered, "was there ever a duller owl?"

"Well, I am going to the library because that's part of our assignment now – to read up on the structure of gales and blizzards and hurricanes. But I'm glad we flew it first. I think it will have more meaning. We're supposed to have a test soon."

"A flying test or a book test?" Gylfie asked.

"Book test. I promised to help Ruby. She's a fantastic flier but she has a hard time with book things – reading and writing."

"Believe me, as long as she can fly that's what counts," Twilight nodded.

"The grand old sage of the Orphan School of Tough Learning!" Gylfie muttered.

Mrs Plithiver gave a slight flinch as she often did when she heard an unkind remark at her tea table. It was then that Soren realised that Mrs Plithiver had barely said a word during the entire teatime. This was most unusual, especially since he had come back so excited from weather chaw. Normally, she would have been thrilled over Soren's enthusiasm. He hoped nothing was the matter. If there was time before good light, after he went to the library, he would go visit her.

Soren flew up to the library humming happily the last verse of the weather chaw song. How quickly life changes, he thought. It was only yesterday that he had returned from walking around with a live coal in his beak, thinking that life could not be much worse – unless, of course, he was in St Aggie's picking pellets in the pelletorium. And now he was a member of the best of the best of the chaws.

When he entered the library he saw Ezylryb in his usual spot with a pile of dried caterpillars. He trotted up to him. "Hello, Ezylryb. It was a wonderful chaw. Do you think there's any chance of another gale coming through soon – or maybe a tornado? Poot says tornadoes are fantastic to fly."

But Ezylryb barely looked up from his book and growled in that unfriendly way he had. Soren took a step back. He was confused. How could Ezylryb be so different now than he had been when they were flying? During weather chaw, Ezylryb had been loud and boisterous and cracking wet poop jokes and singing raucously, and now he was just Ezylryb, a distant, gruff old scholar with his beak buried in a book. "Better study for your test. And Ruby over there needs some help. Flies like a dream but can't spell worth a pellet."

Soren backed away and then turned to Ruby, who was hunched over the book *Weather Systems and Their Structure: How to Fly Them, Analyse Them and Survive Them,* by Ezekiel Ezylryb.

"This is *sooo* hard, Soren! I'll never pass the test."

"Oh, come on, Ruby. You'll do fine. Anyone who flies like you can't flunk a test."

"But it's all these words. I feel flight in my gizzard, but, you know, I can't feel words in my gizzard, except maybe when Madame Plonk sings."

Soren blinked. What Ruby said he thought was probably quite true. "Look, Ruby, I don't think you should try and feel words in your gizzard. You just have to learn a little bit of what they mean in your head – just for the test. Come on, I'll help you. Let's see the book."

Soren took a look. There were a lot of pictures, drawings of storms and hurricanes and blizzards. Soren flipped through the pages with his talon. "Let's start right here with a gale, because that is what we know."

"But what in Glaux's name is a pyte?" Ruby said.

From the corner of the room came a voice. "A pyte is a unit of measurement roughly the wingspan of a Whiskered Screech like meself. It is used for measuring the different structures of a weather system such as gutters, scuppers, et cetera."

"What's et cetera?" whispered Ruby.

"I don't think that's an important word," Soren said. "Now we know what a pyte is, and that's what counts."

Ruby wasn't what Soren would call dumb, but she certainly had terrible handwriting and difficulty with large words. "Finning in the sw…" She read the heading at the top of one page.

"Finning in the swillages," Soren said.

"What is that?" Ruby asked.

"Ruby, you did it. You were the only one who could do it. Don't you remember? You climbed the baggywrinkles out of the scuppers and flew right on the upper edge, twitching your tail. It was very advanced."

"Oh, you mean like this?" And Ruby did a perfect re-creation of what she had done that night.

"Yes, that's it. And it says here that the swillages are measured in tailspans of the individual owl. So if you feel the breeze on either side of your tail at one time you know that it is one tailspan wide."

"Oh, I'll never remember all this! The words, the numbers, it's too much."

"Yes, you will, Ruby."

Otulissa had just come into the library and was pulling out another book on weather interpretation.

"Did you get your chaw changed, Otulissa?" Soren whispered, for he knew she had applied directly to Barran.

Otulissa blinked. Large tears were forming in her eyes. "No! I'm stuck and I can't fly nearly as well as either of you. I'll probably get killed."

For the first time, Soren felt really sorry for Otulissa. Just then a dried caterpillar dropped into the book she had opened.

"You'll do fine, child. Spotted Owls have an amazing talent for sensing pressure changes. Of course, it does make them fussy and hard to live with. I suggest you read that book over there – *Atmospheric Pressures and Turbulations: An Interpreter's Guide.* It was written by Strix Emerilla, a renowned weathertrix of the last century. But I always want a Spotted Owl in my chaw, even if they continually beak off." Ezylryb, with his odd three-taloned walk, hobbled out of the library.

Confound that owl, Soren thought. He is as impenetrable as any weather system. He had hardly spoken to Soren and now seemed to go out of his way to chat it up with Otulissa.

"A Strix wrote this?" Otulissa said as she opened the book. "Oh, my goodness, it could be a relative. And, of course, you know, to become a weathertrix requires the most highly refined sensitivities of all. No wonder a Strix would become one. With our ancient lineage, I would imagine

196

these skills have been honed to perfection through the ages."

Oh, Glaux, does this owl ever shut up? Soren decided to go visit Mrs P before good light.

"Well, I don't know. I just don't know. I don't think I'm sure about anything, really." Soren stopped just outside the small hollow that Mrs P shared with the two other nest snakes. It was the sadness in Mrs P's voice that really stopped him. Mrs P never sounded this way. She was always so positive and full of hope. He listened for a few moments.

"The harp guild is the most prestigious and I think it is my destiny to become a member," the other snake was saying. "You know, the way the owls feel things in their gizzards. Now, I know that we don't have gizzards, but even so."

"Mercy! The very idea." Mrs P sounded genuinely shocked by the suggestion. She spoke sharply now. "I think it is very presumptuous of us to ever think of ourselves as anything like these noble owls. We are not of their station." Now she was sounding like herself again. Mrs P did not have feelings of inferiority. She felt she was the best nest-maid snake ever, but she would never presume, as she said, to think she shared anything with the members of the finest class of birds. Her duty in life was to serve them, and to serve them well was a noble task.

"But Mrs P," the snake continued, "you must have some preference for a guild."

"Oh, it is more than a preference. When we went for our tour of the guilds, I knew immediately that the harp was for me. As I slipped through the strings from one note to another, climbing the scales, leaping octaves, the vibrations never left me. And the very best part was to try to – oh, how shall I explain – weave the music into Madame Plonk's voice. So that together the sound of the harp and the sound of Madame Plonk's voice made something so large and splendid."

Soren blinked. Mrs P, he thought, had something much better than a gizzard.

"Must be off myself," the other nest snake said cheerily. "I'm just going around to drop in on Octavia, bring her a few well-seasoned milkberries. She does love them so and, as you know, she does keep the nest for Madame Plonk. Never can hurt, can it? Ta-ta!" And she slithered out of the hollow.

Soren wedged himself into a corner where he wouldn't be seen. But he heard Mrs P muttering after the other snake was out of earshot. "To presume to have a gizzard and then go slithering off to Octavia, humming tunes and besieging her with milkberries. Well I never!"

Soren decided to skip visiting Mrs P. He knew what he must do. He must 'drop by' Madame Plonk's, and he must tell her that here was a very special snake, a snake that had something even finer than a gizzard, a snake of the highest – what was that word Mrs P was always using? – "sensibilities, artistic sensibilities".

CHAPTER NINETEEN

A Visit to Madame Plonk

"You see, Madame Plonk, I know that perhaps this is not proper – me coming to you this way." Soren could hardly keep his mind on what he was saying, as he had never in his life seen a hollow like this one. The air spun with coloured light from the whirlyglasses that hung from the ceiling and sometimes jutted out from the walls, suspended on twigs jammed into cracks. There were several openings through which light poured. There were pieces of cloth embroidered with beautiful designs and one little niche spilled over with strands of luminous beads. Indeed, the hollow seemed to swirl with colour. And in the middle of all this colour there was a dazzling whiteness – Madame Plonk.

Soren gulped and tried to keep his eyes from straying from that whiteness. "But I just know that Mrs P is rather shy and would never dare."

"Mrs P?" Madame Plonk broke in. "I don't believe I know this snake."

"She came with me, ma'am. She's my family's old nest-maid snake."

"Oh, and you were saying that she wants to be in the harp guild?"

"Yes, ma'am." Soren thought he sounded so stupid. *Who cares?* he thought. He was here for Mrs P. She wanted this so much. Then it was as if Madame Plonk nearly took his next thought directly out of his head.

"But wanting is one thing. One cannot merely want."

"Yes, yes, just because you want something doesn't mean it should always happen."

Madame Plonk blinked and nodded. "Very wise, young'un. But tell me now – why do you think she, this Mrs P as you call her, wants it?"

An idea suddenly popped into Soren's head. "You know," he began thoughtfully, "some snakes might want it just because it is thought of as the most important guild, one for snakes who have served in nests of very old, distinguished families. But I don't think that is why Mrs P wants it."

"No?" Madame Plonk seemed surprised.

Soren had a dreadful feeling that he had said something wrong. He took a deep breath. There was no backing out of it now. "No, I don't think she gives two pellets about that kind of thing."

Madame Plonk blinked.

She's laughing at me, Soren thought. But he continued. "I think she wants to be a member of this guild not because it is the most important but because it is the most artistic."

Madame Plonk gave a little gasp. "That's very interesting. Now what do you mean by artistic, young'un?"

Oh dear, Soren thought. It was as if his gizzard had just dropped out of him. He had no idea what he meant by artistic. But he knew that what he had said was right in some way.

Madame Plonk waited.

Soren continued. "When Mrs P spoke about music she said how when she visited the great harp, she tried to weave the notes not just through the strings of the harp but into your voice. So that together the sound of the harp and the sound of your voice made something that she called splendid and grand. Well, I think that is what it means to be an artist."

There was silence in the apartments. And then Madame Plonk sighed deeply and reached for a hankie made by the lacemakers' guild. She blew her beak and dabbed her eyes. "You are most unusual for a Barn Owl." Soren did not know if that was good or bad. "Now I think you must go. It is almost time for Evensong. So, go along. I hear you're doing quite well in weather chaw." Soren was about to ask how she knew about weather chaw but then remembered that Octavia took care of both Madame Plonk's and Ezylryb's nests. "Now fly along."

"Yes, yes, thank you for your time, Madame Plonk," Soren said, backing out of the hollow.

"Octavia!" Madame Plonk called as soon as Soren had left. "Octavia, come in here immediately."

The fat old nest snake slithered in from a branch where she had hung herself just outside the apartment.

"Did you hear that, Octavia?"

"Yes, ma'am. I think we got ourselves a G-flat!"

CHAPTER TWENTY

Fire!

Ezylryb perched on a limb at the very top of the Great Ga'Hoole Tree and squinted into the blueness of the early summer day. He had been perched here for the last two days almost continuously with Poot by his side. They were studying the cloud behaviour on the far side of Hoolemere.

"Bring the chaw up," he ordered tersely. "There's enough for them to observe."

"What! What!" Soren yawned sleepily as Poot shook him awake. "It's the middle of the day, Poot. We're supposed to be sleeping."

"Not now, young'un. Important lesson, top of the tree. Cap wants you there now. Quick-o!"

What could it be? Soren thought. Poot only called Ezylryb Cap when they were on a flight mission. But there wasn't any bad weather. It was a calm, perfectly clear day. It was the time of the golden rain, when the strands of Ga'Hoole berries that hung from the limbs turned a rich yellow.

By the time Soren got to the top limb, the others had assembled – albeit sleepily. Martin was yawning into the morning sun, but Otulissa was alert and full of questions and already peppering the air with her observations of cloud formations. Ruby yarped her morning pellet and looked to Soren as if she was so sleepy she might pitch forwards off the limb. Just at that moment, Bubo and Elvan arrived. This was the first time Soren had seen Bubo for a while. Presumably, he had been on the reconnaissance mission to The Beaks and, thankfully, returned safely, as had the others.

"Put a mouse in it, Otulissa," Bubo growled and delivered a field mouse headfirst into the talkative owl's beak.

"Thank you, Bubo," Ezylryb said in a low growl and blinked.

"Now, anyone know why we are here?" Ezylryb turned to the owls of the weather chaw. Otulissa's talon immediately shot up even though she could not yet talk with her beak stuffed full of mouse. Soren looked around. This was the first time the three rybs, although Bubo was not officially a ryb, had ever been together with the weather chaw. It was obvious: the days of practising with Bubo's coals from the forge were over. They were now going into a forest fire. A silence fell upon the young owls. They pulled in their feathers tight to their sides. The only sound was Otulissa gulping the last of the mouse. Then, in barely a whisper, her voice shaking with fear, she said, "But I just ate. How shall I ever fly on such a full stomach?"

"Don't worry," Ezylryb said. "We're not flying yet. Not until later. But I want you up here today because you're going to see how fire changes things – the wind, the clouds. You can see these changes even from here. You see, young'uns, there is a fire burning over there across Hoolemere. A great fire." He bobbed out on the branch towards the water. "So later, we shall cross Hoolemere. Then we'll fetch up on some high cliffs on the other side that are perfect for a closer look. We shall camp there for a day or two and then we shall fly in."

For the rest of the morning, they observed the unique behaviour of the clouds on the far side of Hoolemere. The young owls of the weather chaw were used to odd words such as baggywrinkles and scuppers and gutters. But now there were even stranger words as the rybs discussed 'pressure differential', 'thermal inversions' and 'convective columns'.

By mid-afternoon they were dismissed to take a short nap. They would be awakened at tween time, that time between the last drop of sun and the first shadows of twilight, and then take off across Hoolemere.

"Are you nervous, Ruby?" Soren said as they made their way back from the top limbs for their naps.

"I'd be a fool not to be," replied the rusty-feathered owl.

"But you fly so well."

"Not to mention," Martin added, "that both of you are about twice as big as me."

"What are you most scared of?" Soren asked.

"That thing they call crowning," Ruby said quickly. "When the fire leaps from treetop to treetop. I can't imagine what it does to the air. I mean, flying through it must be almost impossible. You could never even half guess where the dead falls might be."

"Technically, the fire does that" – Otulissa had caught up with them – "because the fire climbs what is called, according to the literature, a fuel ladder."

"Yes, and think of me," Martin now spoke. "I am on the ground, supposedly looking for the smallest embers. One of these crowning things happens, and at my weight I get sucked straight up the fuel ladder."

"We all have to spend time on the ground, not just you," Soren said. "It could happen to any of us. You don't have to be little." Martin cocked his head and blinked. He did not look convinced.

Although they had yet to be in an actual forest fire, each member of the chaw had a type of coal or ember they were in charge of gathering. Ruby, being the best flier, would seek airborne embers that were dispersed to the highest parts of the thermal draft columns. Soren and Otulissa were assigned a midpoint position on various sides of the convection column and little Martin was on the ground. But, indeed, they would all have to do a certain amount of groundwork.

Soren could not help but think about how different this flight across Hoolemere was from the time he had crossed the sea to the Great Ga'Hoole Tree nearly six months before. He remembered how the blizzard had raged, how the entire world had turned a swirling white, and the sky and water had melted into one indistinguishable mass. Today the air was clear, the sea below calm with barely a white cap to ruffle the blueness. Seagulls dipped in the last rays of the setting sun. The silvery glint of a fish leaping to escape a larger fish sometimes flashed above the water's surface. Yet as they drew closer to the opposite shore, the air did seem different. And although Soren, like other owls, did not have the keenest sense of smell, the air seemed tinged with an acrid odour.

They landed on the ridge of some high cliffs. Ezylryb was already pointing with his three-taloned foot to some clouds just beyond the ridge. "We call them Ga'Hoole clouds. You know why?"

Otulissa's talon shot up. "Because they are the shape of the seeds found in the Ga'Hoole fruits."

"Right-o, missy," Ezylryb said.

Martin gave a little sigh. "She never stops, does she?"

It was clear that Martin was very nervous. More nervous than the others. Soren felt bad for him. He was the smallest owl in the chaw. It had to be scary. "Don't worry, Martin. You're going to be all right."

"Soren, that's kind of you, but do you realise that I am the first Saw-whet to ever be in the colliering chaw?"

"They must think you're special, Martin," Soren said.

"But what if I'm not?" Martin said, a squeak of desperation creeping into his voice.

Ezylryb continued speaking about the Ga'Hoole clouds. "The reason their tops are curved like that is because – well, you tell me."

Once again, Otulissa's talon shot up. "It's simple weather physics. I was reading about it in Emerilla's, the renowned weathertrix's book – she's a Spotted Owl, I might add." Otulissa cast her eyes downwards in what Soren thought was an outrageously phony show of modesty.

"Just get to the point, darlin'," Ezylryb barked.

"Oh, yes, of course. It is because the winds atop the cloud are blowing much faster than the winds below."

Soren felt Martin begin to tremble. "I might become one of those burning airborne embers that Ruby grabs on the fly," he said in a voice drenched with fear.

"All right now, we camp here and we wait. We wait until the fire is safe for penetration and retrieval. Elvan and Bubo shall take over the mission at that point, directing you to the richest coal and ember beds. I shall remain here and watch the weather and fly in for periodic reports. You do as you're told and no one will get hurt. Ruby and Poot fly top layer. Elvan with Otulissa will be mid-layer. Below them is Soren, who covers Martin on the ground. Bubo and I will be ready if anyone needs help. You are to keep your eye out for your mate."

It was close to midnight when Ezylryb announced that they would be taking off for the next ridge. He had already flown several reconnaissance flights with Poot. He now arrived back on the ridge.

"There's a possible temperature inversion at the east end of the valley. We're not sending any owl down there. Temperature inversions trap smoke, and then do you know what can happen when the smoke starts to rise?" Soren thought that it must mean that the temperature might change, but again, and most annoyingly, Otulissa's talon shot up. "Shut your beak, Otulissa," Ezylryb snapped. "I feel that Soren might have the answer despite not being as deeply familiar as you are with Strix Emerilla."

How does he feel that I have the answer? Is this like being marked – Ezylryb seeing things in me that others can't? But Soren did feel that he knew the answer. So he proceeded tentatively. "I think that it means that when the smoke rises there could be a change in the air." Ezylryb looked straight at him. The light from his yellow eyes did not burn now but seemed to illuminate Soren's entire brain. Soren felt surer, more confident, but mostly he could easily envision the invisible air. "The air would rise and turn and circulate upwards and when this happens, I think the fire will burn harder, more fiercely."

"Exactly!" boomed Ezylryb. "And how do you know this, lad?"

"I see it in my mind. I can imagine it. I feel something, I think in my gizzard, about the movement of air and heat and..."

"Yes, thank you, lad." Ezylryb turned to the other owls of the chaw. "There are many ways to learn – through books, through practice and through gizzuition. They are all good ways, but few of us have gizzuition."

"But what is gizzuition?" Otulissa asked warily.

Ezylryb began to speak but kept his gaze on Soren. "It is a kind of thinking beyond the normal reasoning processes by which one immediately apprehends the truth, perceives and understands reality. It cannot really be taught, but it can be developed by being extremely attentive and sensitive to the natural world."

Soren blinked. I AM something in this old owl's eyes. I am almost as smart as Otulissa, and Ezylryb believes in me!

It was now time to move to a ridge closer to the fire. The chaw lifted into the air, each owl flying close to its buddy. They were not halfway to the next ridge

They had not flown very far before they felt the heat on their faces. They had anticipated the heat but not the noise. A monster roar raged in their ears. Soren had never heard anything like it. Bubo and Elvan had prepared them for everything but this noise. They knew about the heat. They knew about the violent updrafts, the so-called cool spots, and the dead falls. They even knew about the most dreaded trick fire could pull – fire blinking. This happened when the fire, raging with all its deadly beauty, actually transfixed an owl so that it could not fly. It went yeep and, with its wings locking, the owl lost its instincts to fly and suddenly plummeted to the ground. Or if the owl was already on the ground and the fire began to spread rapidly towards it, the owl simply could not lift off, for its wings hung still and motionless like dead things by its side. But no one had told him about the noise.

"You'll get used to it." Elvan had flown up just over Soren and Martin. "It's always a shock at first. There is no way to describe it." He had to shout over the roar of the fire. Below, a sheet of flame lay flat against a hillside. The thermal drafts came up like slabs of rock. Martin and Soren were sucked up at least twenty feet but as they passed the hill they felt a terrific coolness and they dropped another thirty feet.

Soren realised that it was only cool compared to the heat they had just flown through. Bubo now circled back. He had been flying far out in front. "Good ember beds ahead. Perfect for all of you."

So this was it, Soren thought. *This was when they became true colliers.* Just then, like a shooting star, something red whizzed by.

"Beautiful catch, Ruby, " shouted Poot.

"What a natural that Short-eared Owl is!" Elvan gasped in amazement.

Ruby began to wing off towards the coal buckets that Bubo had set up on the ridge. The small buckets made in his forge, with bits of kindling in the bottom already lit, would keep the coals hot.

"All right, Martin going in!" Elvan called out the command. The little owl began a tight spiralling plunge to earth. "Cover him, Soren."

Soren would fly cover until Martin returned with a beakful of cinders. Elvan actually carried the very small cinder pot in his talons. Martin was supposed to not only collect cinders but report back on the larger coals that Soren and Otulissa were to retrieve.

Soren hovered above with a careful eye on the little owl. He was getting used to the noise. Indeed, not only was he getting used to it but within the thunderous roar he could seek out smaller sounds, like the sound of Martin's beating heart, which grew more rapid as he plunged. As Martin's heartbeat quickened, Soren hoped with all his heart, gizzard and soul that the little Saw-whet Owl would be all right. He could see now that Martin was on the ground.

"Play your position, Otulissa," Elvan rasped. Ruby had just caught another sparking coal.

"But all the good ones go up there. We never get a chance."

"Shut your beak. You want to be sent back to the ridge? You'll have your chance."

But Soren was not paying any attention to them. He must keep his focus on Martin, who was now just a little smudge on the ground. A cloud of smoke temporarily obscured him and Soren flew lower.

There he was! There he was! Good heavens, he was coming up fast!

"He's coming in loaded!" Bubo slid in next to Elvan.

And then he was there. Cinders poured from his small beak. His face was sooty and smudged but his eyes danced with a light as bright as the fire. "I did it! I did it!"

"You certainly did, young'un." Bubo flew up and tousled Martin's head feathers with his talon.

"I can't wait to go back," Martin shouted.

"Hold on there," Elvan said. "First, your report."

"Embers about the size of pellets uphill from where I landed."

"Excellent," Elvan said. Elvan then flew off to confer with Bubo and Ezylryb.

"Soren, there is nothing like it. I can't tell you. As soon as I got there I just wasn't frightened at all. And I can't describe what it's like to grab the cinders in your beak. It's…"

"Intoxicating," Otulissa broke in. "Yes, I read about it. You must be careful, though. Strix Emerilla wrote that some colliers get so drunk on the cinders that they do not heed weather warnings."

"Well, it's very strange the feeling you get when you grab them and then fly with them. It's something," he paused. "Something very powerful."

"Now's the time, Soren. You're going in!" Elvan ordered.

"What about me?" Otulissa wailed.

"Shut your beak, your turn will come," Bubo yelled.

Soren pitched into a spiralling downwards twist. He felt himself buffeted by a sudden fierce updraft, but he had gathered enough speed to bore through it. Then he was on the ground. It was a strange landscape. Charred skeletons of trees clawed the night, and then scattered about were the coals like hot glowing rocks. They were told to work quickly but at the same time not to rush. A steady pace is the best pace, Bubo had told them. How had Martin, so little, done it and found cinders perfectly sized for his beak? Great Glaux, how embarrassing it would be, Soren thought, if he could not find embers, if he came back empty-beaked. Bubo and Elvan had tried to emphasise that no one should be embarrassed. Oftentimes in the beginning a young collier did not find a suitable coal. There was no shame in returning empty-beaked. But Soren knew there was.

Suddenly Soren heard a terrible cracking sound. The flames turned a stand of trees just in front of him into one immense torch. He looked up and saw the crowns of other trees igniting. *Crown fire!* Ruby's worse fear. But Ruby had been worried about the air above and now here he was below. He began to feel a mighty pull on him. Was he going to be sucked up? The last thing Soren remembered thinking about clearly was himself turning into a feathery ball of embers. A thought raced through his head: *with my luck, I'll be caught by Otulissa. What will it matter? I'll be dead.*

CHAPTER TWENTY-ONE

"A Coal in My Beak!"

I have a coal in my beak! I have a coal in my beak! The words kept running through Soren's head. He was flying in ascending circles, effortlessly. He was not singed. He was not burning, and there was this wonderful glowing thing in his beak that, indeed, seemed to flood his entire being with an extraordinary feeling. It was as if every single one of his hollow bones, every feather shaft brimmed with this feeling of transcendent power. Joy filled him, a joy such as he had never felt since perhaps the first time he had ever flown. But how he got this coal was still a mystery to him. He flew back to the ridge where the buckets were. Martin was beside him.

"You were spectacular, Soren. I was so nervous when I saw that crown fire break and then when we saw you getting sucked up, I nearly went yeep."

"But what happened?" Soren asked. They were to stay on the ridge until the rest of the chaw returned.

"You mean to tell me you don't know?"

"Not exactly."

"You did a reverse loop to escape the pull and as you were coming out of it this coal flew by. Bubo said he never saw a coal of that size go up so high, but you caught it! Caught it on the loop, Soren. I mean it was better flying than anything Ruby has ever done. It was absolutely spectacular."

"Great Glaux, I wish I'd seen it," Soren said.

Martin hooted loudly. "You did it, Soren! You did it!"

Otulissa flew in next with Ruby and Poot. She had a full beak and dumped the coals into the bucket. "I got one! I got one!" And then she stopped and looked up, genuinely modest now. "But, Soren, it is nothing compared to what you did."

"Well, thank you, Otulissa... er... uh... that is very kind of you."

Otulissa bobbed her head and actually said nothing for once. Martin blinked at Soren as if to say, "I wonder how long that will last?"

Soren looked about for Ezylryb. He wondered if Ezylryb had seen him. Just then, the Whiskered Screech alighted with a bucket. He barely looked at Soren but busied himself shifting some of the coals into the new bucket.

Oh, no, Soren thought. *Will I ever understand this owl?*

Ezylryb was making his way down the line of buckets now. As he came next to the bucket where Soren had dropped his coal, he turned to look at him. The coal he held in his beak cast an eerie glow on his whiskered face. His amber eyes appeared red. "I hear you did a fair night's work," he mumbled through the coal. Then added, "Magnificent, perhaps." He dropped the coal in the bucket and flew off to confer with Poot.

They began their homeward journey with just an hour to spare before First Light. "Don't worry about crows and mobbing," Elvan said. "They never come near when we're carrying live coals."

It was a beautiful time to fly. The air grew fresher and a light wind now ruffled the water into lacy crests. Even now, with the coals and cinders tame in the buckets, their power seemed to touch them. Fire, of course, was perhaps the most important element that made the Great Ga'Hoole Tree different from any other kingdom of owls. It made them more than a community or a gathering of owls. It made them a fellowship. And if they were to rise each night into the blackness and perform noble deeds, it was perhaps the fire that helped them do this: fire punched up to fierce heats with Bubo's bellows for forging metals into battle claws; fire tamed into candle flames for reading and learning. And here these young owls of the chaw, just barely finished with being owlets themselves, were flying back across the Sea of Hoolemere with this precious element. No wonder they felt powerful. And now, as the sun rose bloodred in the east, Bubo's deep rumble began to ring out across the water. It was the song of the colliers.

Give me a hot coal glowing bright red,
Give me an ember sizzling with heat,
These are the jewels made for my beak.
We fly between flames and never get singed
We plunge through the smoke and never cringe.
The secrets of fire, its strange winds, its rages,
We know it all as it rampages
Through forests, through canyons,
Up hillsides and down.
We'll track it.

We'll find it.
Take coals by the pound.
We'll yarp in the heart of the hottest flame
Then bring back its coals and make them tame.
For we are the colliers brave beyond all
We are the owls of the colliering chaw!

They arrived shortly after daybreak at the Great Ga'Hoole Tree, their faces smudged, their beaks sooty black. But they were welcomed as heroes. The coals were delivered to Bubo's forge and then there was a great banquet.

"Where's Twilight?" Soren said as he sat down with Gylfie at Mrs Plithiver's table. "And Primrose?" Soren wanted to tell Twilight about the forest fire. Few things impressed Twilight but this might.

"They're both out on a mission and so is Digger. They needed the tracking and search-and-rescue chaws. Something big's going on," Gylfie said.

"What?"

"I'm not sure exactly. Boron is being very quiet about it. But suddenly a lot of owlets need rescuing fast." Just then, he saw Ezylryb huddled with Boron and Strix Struma in a corner of the dining hollow. They looked terribly serious, and he saw Ezylryb nodding quickly every now and then. Poot started to approach the three owls and he was immediately shooed away.

Because Ezylryb had not taken up his usual position with Elvan at the head of Octavia, the weather and colliering table was empty. Martin and Ruby had joined Soren and Gylfie at Mrs P's, along with Otulissa. "Thank goodness we can now have our vole roasted," Otulissa said. "It seems like forever since we've had anything cooked."

"I would have thought you would have had your fill of things roasting after flying into that fire," Mrs P said, and they all laughed. "Now I have a little announcement to make." The old nest-maid snake spoke softly.

"What is it, Mrs P?" Soren asked.

"Well, I have been asked to join the Harp Guild."

"Oh, Mrs P!" they all cried.

Perhaps Soren's visit to Madame Plonk had counted for something. He had dared not even hope ever since he had visited her extraordinary apartments that day. Soren couldn't have been happier. *Everything,* he thought, *is really perfect.* But as soon as he thought of the word 'perfect', he realised no, not quite. And once more that strange melancholy feeling began to creep like a mist over him. He knew what it was immediately this time. Eglantine. What had happened to his dear baby sister? He supposed that if she were alive, and if she had not been captured by St Aggie's or something worse, she would be flying by now. But who would ever see her? Not his parents. Who knew if they were still alive? Soren grew very quiet. Mrs P sensed his sadness.

"Come up later, Soren dear, and sit with me a spell and tell me all about your adventures in the burning forest."

"Sure, Mrs P," he said distractedly.

But he didn't. He was simply too tired from the flight, the work at the fire, to do anything but go right to sleep. He was so tired he did not even hear the beautiful voice of Madame Plonk. And underneath the voice that morning there was an especially lovely rippling sound, almost liquid, as Mrs Plithiver slid with a steady pressure very quickly from the midpoint on a string and stretched for the next octave, all the way to G-flat. It was a virtuoso move and Madame Plonk knew that she had made the right decision. This Mrs P had a maestro's touch to match her own magnificent voice.

But, of course, Soren slept through it all, dreaming perhaps of his little sister, but perhaps he was even too tired for dreams.

CHAPTER TWENTY-TWO

Owlets Down!

While Soren slept, in a distant wood across the Sea of Hoolemere, Twilight swooped through the gathering gloom at the end of the day. He and Primrose and Digger worked together. Digger, of course, as part of the tracking chaw, did the groundwork, looking for telltale pellets, a fluff of down, or sometimes a wounded or dead owlet. Primrose, who was in the search-and-rescue chaw along with Twilight, flew all levels as an outrider and kept a sharp lookout for enemies. Twilight did most of the heavy work of lifting the owlets and when possible restoring them to their nests.

This particular mission had started as what Barran described as routine. But it quickly became something much more complicated. In the first reconnaissance wave, a number of owlets had been reported on the ground, but they did not seem to be near their nests. At first the rescuers thought these owls, stunned and cold, had simply forgotten where their nests were, which trees they had fallen from. But then it became apparent that in the nearby trees there were no hollows, no possible nests for these young owls. So where had they come from? Had they been snatched by St Aggie's patrols and then, in flight, somehow mutinied and escaped the talons of their captors, falling to the ground? But why would St Aggie's patrols not retrieve them? It was all quite mystifying. The other thing that was peculiar was that they were all Barn Owls, not just *Tyto alba* like Soren, but Masked Owls and Grass Owls and Sooty Owls, all belonging to the Barn Owl family.

Twilight divided his attention between Digger below and Primrose, who was flying over him. He had retracted his battle claws, because there did not seem to be any St Aggie's agents around and it was necessary to pull them in when picking up a fallen owlet, so as not to hurt it. Another Great Grey was wearing his battle claws fully extended and circling in case of ambush. They traded off. This was how the search-and-rescue chaw operated – in pairs, with one owl flying in full battle suit while the other was prepared to pick up an owlet in distress. When one was found, it was taken to a gathering spot in a large hollow presided over by one of Barran's assistants, who could administer medical attention before flying the owls back to the Great Ga'Hoole Tree. When there were enough owlets gathered, they set off. But now there were more than enough. That was why backup had been requested. More of everything was needed. More search-and-rescue workers, more assistants at the gathering spots, more trackers. It was an almost overwhelming situation. Never had they dealt with so many nestless owlets. Where were their parents? Where were their hollows? They seemed to have dropped out of nowhere.

Twilight spotted a Sooty Owl on the ground. This was the most difficult time of the day for owls to spot downed owlets. And Sooties were the most difficult of all owls to spot. Neither black nor white but a smudgy ash colour, they seemed to blend in with the twilight. But Twilight himself, with his peculiar gift for seeing at this time, was well suited for the task. Making sure his battle claws were locked back, he began a quick plunge. He hoped the little fellow wasn't dead.

Cautiously he poked it with his beak. He detected a heartbeat. Then gently he scooped it up in his talons. It stirred a bit and tried to lift its head. He thanked Glaux, there was life in this one. There was nothing worse than picking up a dead owlet. Despite their small size, they seemed to be especially heavy, and if their eyes weren't closed and they were dead, it was awful! Barran had not expected that they would encounter any dead owlets on their first mission. She was very upset for the new members of the chaw. "It wasn't supposed to be like this," she kept saying.

"Now you take it easy, little Sooty," Twilight spoke gently to the owlet. "We're going to get you nice and fixed up. Don't you worry. You're in the talons of a champ here!" Twilight couldn't resist a little exhibition of his finer flight manoeuvre. Besides, an owlet might find them comforting.

Hush little owl,
You're with Twi.
I got the moves to get you by.
Big bad crows.
St Aggie's scamps
Ain't got nothin to show this champ.
I'll pop a spiral
With a twist,
Do a three-sixty
And scatter mist—

*   *   *

In the middle of what Twilight considered one of the finest poetry compositions he had ever made midair, the little Sooty began to make a sound like a weak whistle.

"My Tyto, my Tyto, why hast thou forsaken us in our purity?"

Twilight looked down at the limp little Sooty in his talons. "What are you talking about? Forsaken? You call this forsaken? Look, I'm not Glaux but you're safe right here in my talons. Safer than you were down on the ground." But the little Sooty just stared at him with vacant dark eyes.

Strix Struma was suddenly on his upwind side. "Don't be upset, Twilight. All these owlets are babbling some kind of nonsense. It's all very weird. This is not like what they did at St Aggie's with the moon-blinking business, but it's strange. Very strange talk all the time about Tyto. Bubo and Boron are on their way and Ezylryb is coming as well."

"Ezylryb?" Twilight was surprised. Ezylryb never left the Great Ga'Hoole Tree, except for forest fires and weather interpretation. A lot of owlets falling out of nowhere didn't seem to be a weather situation or a forest fire.

"We need all the help we can get and not just for the rescue. Something's going on out here and we must get to the bottom of it." What Strix Struma did not add was that it was for precisely this reason that they needed Ezylryb. Only Ezylryb, with his immense knowledge gleaned from years of reading and his long life of experiences throughout every owl kingdom, might be able to begin to understand what was going on here. Strix Struma was as worried as she had ever been. Was it a plague of some sort? A spell? A bewitchment? She didn't believe in such nonsense. She broke off these thoughts. "Get that Sooty back to the gathering spot and then if you have it in you and feel you could fly one more mission, do so." She sheered off downwind.

"All this talk about purity and Tytos. Never heard such a bunch of babble in my life." It was Elsie, a rather bunchy-looking Barred Owl, who seemed to have more feathers than her small body could manage. The bar designs on her wings had almost faded into a blur. But she was a kindly old bird who, along with Matron, was in charge of the care and feeding of all the newly arrived young owlets at the Great Ga'Hoole Tree. Never before had the two owls actually been brought out to a gathering station on a search-and-rescue mission, however.

"Over here, Twilight," Matron called. "I have just fluffed up a place. That Sooty will fit in nicely.

Elsie dear, spare me a bit more down for this Sooty."

Elsie obliged by plucking out some downy fluff from beneath her primaries. Twilight blinked. It was just as Elsie said. A low babble came in a steady stream from the little owlets, and they were all reciting some kind of poetry, and it made absolutely no sense to Twilight.

One little Grass Owl was now chanting in a thin little voice, "Tytos now forever, so pure, so rare! Yet supreme!" A Masked Owl spoke of a Tyto to whom righteousness belonged and still another was crying out, "Oh, Tyto, who is pureness beyond compare, show thyself... Tyto, how long shall the impure triumph?"

"Depressing little ditties, aren't they?" Bubo said as he lighted down next to Twilight.

"What are they talking about?" Twilight said.

"I don't know, but I've heard more cheerful tunes in my day than all this whining about Tytos."

As Twilight and Primrose and Digger took off for their last mission, the ragtag ends of mournful songs seemed to trail out behind them. "My goodness," sighed Primrose. "It's enough to make you long for a nice little wet poop joke." She dropped down to her mid-level surveillance position, and then Digger flew under her. It was well beyond the last of the daylight. It was night. No longer flying on that silver border, Twilight would wait for signals from Primrose or Digger if they found any owlets down. Digger now swooped in close to the ground. In the muddy runoff from a creek, he saw the distinctive markings of a Barn Owl's front talons, the toes exactly equal lengths. He followed the talon marks down the muddy path. Perhaps this one was not injured so badly if it could walk, Digger thought. But where could it have walked? And why? He saw a buff-coloured feather in the path ahead. A feather of an almost fully fledged owl, it would seem. So why not fly? And just within that moment, under the low branches of a juniper, he saw a tawny glow in the night and he heard the long, drawn-out hiss, the begging call of a Tyto alba. "Coo coo ROOOO! Coo coo ROOOO!"

Digger hooted the signal indicating a downed owlet.

As Digger waited for Twilight to spiral down, the strangest feeling began to steal over him. Twilight settled down next to him.

"What have we got here?" Twilight said.

"Another Barn Owl, but not a Masked or a Sooty or a Grass Owl."

"No," Twilight said in a whisper. "A *Tyto alba.*"

"Like Soren," they both said at once. Digger looked at Twilight. He almost didn't dare say it. "Do you think it could be?"

"Remember," Twilight said, "how Soren once told us that his sister had a speckle near her eye. That it looked as if one of those dots from her head feathers had just slipped down to her eye and that it was the same with his mother, that she too had a slipped dot?"

"Yes," said Digger slowly.

"Look!"

The two owls brought their beaks close to the little owl, whose cries had grown weaker and weaker and then stopped. They almost forgot to breathe in their anguish. There was indeed a tiny speckle in the darker feathers on the inside corner of her eye. But if this was Eglantine, was she alive? Was she dead? Was she truly...?

"Eglantine?" they both called softly.

CHAPTER TWENTY-THREE

At Last!

"I need some more worms over here, quick!" the nest-maid snake called out.

"The Ga'Hoolology chaw is digging them as fast as they can," another snake called. "Oh, my goodness, what a mess this little Sooty Owl is." The snake nudged the last worm of her supply on the gash in the Sooty's wing. "Poor little fellow. Now stop that babbling, dear. You don't have enough energy." But the owlet kept up a steady singsong about a world of Tyto purity and supremacy.

There had never been such a flurry in the Great Ga'Hoole Tree. The infirmary was brimming with stunned and wounded owls. And no one was spared a moment's rest. The owls of the tree were cutting back and forth between branches, flying in the new arrivals, rushing about getting fresh worms for their wounds, plucking down from their own breasts to make up new beds, bringing cup after cup of milkberry tea. The nest-maid snakes were at the point of complete exhaustion and even Madame Plonk, who rarely lifted a talon around the tree to do anything, could not bear seeing her harp guild so worn out. So she joined in right beside them, learning how to place worms properly on the open wounds. Soren and Gylfie worked as hard as anyone, either fetching things for the nest-maid snakes or cleaning out new hollows, because the infirmary was too full to accommodate any more. There was barely time to wonder about what had brought this on. But, of course, in the back of their minds was the horrible nagging fear that St Aggie's was somehow involved, and if not St Aggie's, perhaps the 'you only wish'! Were the poor little owls babbling about the same horror as the murdered Barred Owl when he gasped the words 'you only wish'? But what did it really matter? Owlets were wounded and dying.

For the life of him, Soren could not understand this babble that seemed to pour out of the owlets' ceaselessly clacking beaks. It never seemed as if there was an entire phrase. The words came out disjointed and broken, but always there was something about Tytos or Barn Owls.

Then overhead, Soren heard the arrival of a new batch of owlets being brought in. There was no quiet flying this day. Owls that once prided themselves on silent flight beat their wings furiously, in their desperate efforts to get the injured owlets to safety.

"SOREN!" The sound of his own name split the warm air. Soren looked up from his task of pecking out worms. It was Twilight who had called down to him and he was flanked by Primrose and Digger. The rest of the search-and-rescue chaw was following.

"Soren, get up here fast as you can," Twilight called again.

Then Digger spiralled down. "This is important. Bring that worm and come on."

"No! No!" another owl said tersely. "All worms must be put into the pile first. Our chaw ryb said so."

"Drop the worm, Soren, and just come." Soren couldn't imagine what could be so important that they needed him so quickly. He followed Digger to a new hollow they had just fixed up to take care of the overflow from the infirmary. Outside the hollow, Gylfie and Primrose perched on a branch. They were very still. Soren got an awful feeling in his gizzard. He hesitated. He really did not want to go into that hollow. Digger gave him a bit of a nudge. Then Gylfie came up on the other side. The shadows from the hollow seemed to draw him in against his will. He blinked. Twilight stood beside a heap of golden feathers splotched with blood.

"So?" Soren said.

Twilight's usually gruff voice became a soft whisper. "So, Soren, is this your sister, Eglantine?"

Soren felt his gizzard drop to his talons. He wobbled but Gylfie was on one side and Digger on the other. He forced himself to look down at the battered little owlet. But she really was hardly an owlet any more. She was fully fledged and streaked with blood. A red bubble burbled from her beak as she too tried to babble.

"No! No! This can't be!" Soren wailed. He felt his legs collapse under him and he crumpled beside her. "Eglantine! Eglantine!"

"Get Mrs Plithiver, quick!" Gylfie rasped.

Time began to have no meaning for Soren. Was it day? Was it night? How many nights had passed since they had brought in Eglantine? At first he was numb. He could not do anything. Mrs Plithiver nursed Eglantine ceaselessly. "Will she live?" That was all Soren could say.

"I'm not sure, dear," Mrs P said honestly. "All we can do is try."

Finally, Soren began to help. He tried feeding her a bit of milkberry tea and in a low voice kept saying, "Eglantine, it's me, Soren. It's your brother Soren." But Eglantine, with her eyes half shut, only continued to babble a word or two of the singsong ditties they all sang. She did seem to be getting better, however, stronger. And when her eyes opened fully, Soren grew excited. "Eglantine!" He leaned over her. "Eglantine. It's me. Soren! And Mrs P is here too!" But there was not even a flicker of recognition in her eyes. She merely clacked her beak a couple of times and resumed the babble. Soren sighed.

"Patience, dear. Patience," said Mrs Plithiver. "All things take time. See how much stronger her voice is."

But Soren did not like what he was hearing. She spoke only of Tytos, of Tytos reigning supreme, seeking vengeance, of Tyto purity, of Tyto superiority, of a world only of Tytos. How would he explain to her that his best friends were an Elf Owl, a Great Grey and a Burrowing Owl? That these were his very best friends in all the world, that they were a band?

By the next evening, Eglantine was well enough to get up on her talons and take a few steps. Soren led her carefully out on the branch and stood beside her. But he might as well have been standing beside a stump. She did whatever he told her, but there was still no recognition. He brought her into the hollow he shared with Twilight, Digger and Gylfie to sleep, and Primrose came just before Madame Plonk began her song, to show Eglantine some especially pretty berries she had strung.

"See, Eglantine. Ever since I have been here, I have collected a few berries from each season. So I have white ones from winter and silver from spring and now I've got my golden ones from summer, and I'm making a necklace. I'll make you one too." But Eglantine did not respond.

"This is worse than being moon blinked," Soren whispered to Gylfie.

Gylfie didn't know what to say. She felt desperately sorry for Soren. She knew that Soren had missed Eglantine so fiercely. But to have her back like this was almost worse than not having her back at all. Gylfie, of course, would never dare say such a thing to Soren. Just then Otulissa peeked her head in.

"May I come in?"

"Sure," Soren said.

"Look, I've been in the library all this time working on Tyto research, to see if there is anything that would explain this – all of them being Tytos and babbling about Tytos, but I somehow got distracted and started looking at a book by a distinguished Spotted Owl that's about owls' brains and feelings and gizzards."

"Great Glaux," Twilight muttered and yarped a pellet out the hollow's opening. "No doubt a relative of yours, Otulissa."

"Well, possibly. There were many distinguished intellects in our ancestry and we do go back so far. Anyhow, in this book it says that your sister might be suffering from something he calls 'gizzlemia'. It is a blankness of the gizzard. It is as if the gizzard is just walled off and nothing can get through, and because of this there is a malfunction in the brain as well."

"Well, that explains so much," Soren said sarcastically. "What in Glaux's name am I supposed to do about it?"

"Well… well," Otulissa stammered. "I'm not sure. I just thought you'd like to know what's making her this way. It's not as if she doesn't want to remember you. She just can't help it," Otulissa said feebly. "I… I mean… I'm sure she loves you still." Soren stared at her with a hard glint. "Oh, dear. None of this is coming out right." Otulissa's eyes welled with tears. "I was just trying to be helpful."

Soren just sighed, turned away and began to fluff up the bed they had made for Eglantine.

That day, as the darkness leaked away into the morning and the light of morning turned harsh in the glare of noon, in that hot slow time of the day when the silence pressed down despite the babble, Soren felt as lonely as he had ever felt in his life. Lonelier than that first frightening night on the ground when he had been pushed out of the nest by his brother, Kludd, lonelier than when he had been at St Aggie's, lonelier than when he had almost given up on ever seeing any of his family again. This was the most excruciating loneliness he had ever imagined. Eglantine was here at last, but was she really?

CHAPTER TWENTY-FOUR

Trader Mags

Soren had been looking forward, it seemed forever, to the day that Trader Mags would come with her wares. But now it meant nothing to him. Still, there was certainly a buzz of excitement as they roused themselves at the end of the day in anticipation of the magpie's arrival around twilight. Everyone was excited except for Soren and, of course, the nest-maids, who considered magpies among the worst of the wet poopers, almost as bad as seagulls. He supposed he would go and drag Eglantine around, although he doubted it would mean anything to her. Mags would be showing her wares all evening, so there was no rush.

She was late and no one was more upset than Madame Plonk. From his hollow, Soren could hear her several branches above him on a lookout perch, waiting with other owls. "If that bird was ever on time in her life, I'll eat my harp!" Madame Plonk was fuming. "She has no sense of time. Here it is past twilight, nearly First Black." But suddenly, curling out of the night, came a lovely warbling sound.

"It's the carol!" someone shouted. And a cheer went up. Mags was approaching and her carolling threaded through the night. The warble of magpies was known as a carol and was like no other birdsong in the world. He heard the owls now, swooping down through the branches to the base of the tree where Mags would set up her wares. She came with several assistants, carrying baskets of her latest "collection", as she called her wares.

"Want to go down, Eglantine?" Soren said. Eglantine, of course, said nothing but got up and followed Soren. She had recovered her flight skills almost immediately and the two alighted on the ground together as Mags and her assistants spread out the collection.

There was a festive mood with much chattering and special treats that cook had whipped up. Bubo stomped forwards and gave Mags a great hug with his wings that nearly knocked her over. Mags looked nothing like Soren had expected. Her feathers were mostly black and the sleekest, blackest black he had ever seen, but she did have some streaks of white feathers. Her tail was immensely long and, on this moonlit night, her black tail feathers had a greenish gloss. She wore a jaunty bandanna on her head. "More where these came from, my dears!" she squawked. Soren could have been knocked over by that squawk. How could the same throat that produced that lovely carol be squawking as raucously as a seagull?

"Come on up, don't be shy," Mags said. "Bubbles, Bubbles!" she squawked at a smaller magpie. "Where're them sparklies I got at the whatchama-callit for Madame? You know the ones. And I got you some nice velvet, dear," nodding to Madame Plonk. "Ever so squashy. Tassels, tassels anyone? Tie some crystals to them and yeh got yerself a charming windchime... Bubbles! Get them crystals out here on the double! I tell you, Boron, you can't get a good apprentice these days. I mean one would think that to serve Mags the Trader, known from here to Tyto, from Kuneer to Ambala, would be enough incentive, if you catch my drift, but no. How's the missus, now where she be?"

"Away," Boron said cryptically.

The little black eye almost covered by the bandanna gave a quick piercing stare. "Oh," she said. Then muttered to herself as Boron walked away. "I just mind me own business. I don't ask no questions, don't butt my beak in where it ain't wanted."

"Ha!" Bubo laughed. "If that ain't a pile of yarped pellets."

"Oh scram, Bubo," she replied merrily. "Get out of here with your yarping pellet talk. Remember, we're not fit to associate with you, we wet poopers."

"Now, Maggie. I ain't no snob and you know it. I never held that against you. I mean, you're different from seagulls, sweet gizzard."

"Don't you go 'sweet gizzarding' me, Bubo. And I'll say we're different from seagulls. About twice as smart and ten times prettier. Not as pretty as Madame Plonk, though, in that gorgeous tapestry piece I found for her." She flew over and began to help Madame Plonk arrange it more artfully on her high white shoulders.

Soren felt Eglantine flinch. "You OK, Eglantine?" She said nothing but he noticed that she had turned towards Madame Plonk, who was admiring herself in a fragment of mirror that Mags had brought.

They had moved on. Walking along, they looked at other simpler cloths that had been spread with a variety of items – a bright pocket watch, several broken saucers with a sign that said "mendable", a strange flower that Soren paused to look at. "It ain't real," the little magpie, Bubbles, said.

"Well, if it isn't real, what is it?" Soren asked.

"It's an unreal flower," Bubbles answered.

"But why have an unreal flower?"

"It ain't never gonna die. Ya see?"

Soren didn't see but moved along. Despite all the merriment, he noticed that Boron and Strix Struma were always huddled together in tense conversation. They seemed, in fact, very apart from the entire festive spirit of the evening.

Soon Soren and Eglantine joined Twilight and Digger and Primrose. Primrose had traded one of her strung milkberry bracelets for a tiny comb. And Digger had traded a very smooth pebble for a shell. "They say it comes from a very faraway ocean and that once a tiny animal lived inside it," he explained.

The moon was beginning to slip away and Mags had begun to pack up her wares. It would be time for good light, but suddenly Soren noticed that Eglantine was not by his side. He had a terrible moment's panic but then spotted her standing rigidly in front of a cloth covered with fragments of glass and pretty stones.

Bubbles was packing up. "She ain't moved an inch," Bubbles said. "Just staring at this stone here, with the sparkles. Ain't really gold, Mags says – just little bits of something she calls isinglass, some calls it mica. But makes a right pretty rock. Kind of sparkly in places and, if you hold it up, light can shine through it a bit. It's kind of like a dusty mirror. Certainly caught your sister's fancy. There be something wrong with her, I s'pose?" she said quietly to Soren. "Here, dear, I'll show you something real pretty we can do with it." She picked up the stone, which was as thin as a blade. "See what it does now." She held it up to the moon as it swept down on the dark horizon. When the light of the moon touched the stone it grew luminous. At that very same moment, the harp could be heard as the guild began their evening practice. No one else noticed, of course, but for one fraction of a second the stone blade shimmered in a swirl of flickering light and sound.

Eglantine began to shake uncontrollably. "The Place! The Place!" Eglantine screamed.

Something started in a dim way to make sense to Soren. He put a talon on his sister's shoulder and spun her around to face him. "Eglantine," he said softly.

His sister blinked. "Soren? Oh, Soren!" she cried as he swept her under his wings.

"I ain't done nothing, Mags, I swear. Nothing." Bubbles was crying and sputtering in near hysterics. "I just held up this here piece of glass we got from that castle over in Ambala and she done gone yoicks."

"Take me to the music, Soren. Take me to the music. Take us all to the music," Eglantine cried.

CHAPTER TWENTY-FIVE

In the Folds of the Night

Soren perched on a slender branch next to Eglantine. He draped one wing over her shoulders. It seemed like a miracle. His sister was back – really back. And now she said they must listen to the harp music. If she had told him to hang upside down and be mobbed by crows, he would have. He had never been happier in his life. The other owlets that had been rescued were now gathering on the limbs outside the concert hollow. Madame Plonk rarely allowed owls to observe harp practice but she made an exception now. Boron came and perched on the other side of Eglantine. They all watched as the nest-maid snakes of the guild gathered at the harp and took their positions. Half of the guild snakes played the higher strings and the other half played the lower strings, and then there were a very few, the most talented harp snakes, that were called sliptweens. The job of the sliptweens was to jump octaves. An octave contained all eight tones of the scale. This harp had six and a half octaves, from C-flat below middle C to the G-flat. G-flat was three and a half octaves above middle C. To find a snake that could do that jump and do it well in a split second, causing the most beautiful liquid sound to pour from the harp, was rare. And it could be exhausting work, depending on the composition.

Mrs P was a natural sliptween. And Soren now blinked as he saw a pink streak pass through the strings of the harp and a beautiful sound drifted into the air. It was Mrs P. Then in a flash she was back in her original position, weaving bass notes. It was lovely to watch. Not only was the music magnificent but the snakes themselves, in their varying hues of rosy pinks, wove a continually shifting pattern as they shuttled through the strings of the harp.

They were now playing an old forest cantata. And Madame Plonk's voice blended perfectly with the sounds of the harp.

Soren looked at Eglantine. She had a relaxed, dreamy look in her eyes. All of the rescued owlets seemed different now. There was not one clack of a babbling beak. The owls were silent and happy.

Boron had been watching them all from a higher perch. He was deeply perplexed. Happy, of course, that all the owls they had rescued had stopped their babbling. But mystified as to how it had happened. Beyond Hoole, he sensed that there was a danger lurking that was worse than the owls of St Aggie's. And why had Ezylryb not returned yet? Barran had come back during the harp practice, but she was surprised that Ezylryb was not yet back. She thought he had a head start on her. "Don't worry, dear. He'll show up."

Soren looked at Boron and Barran. Despite their words, they did seem worried. And Soren himself had a funny feeling in his gizzard. Gylfie suddenly turned to him.

"I think they're worried about Ezylryb."

Soren blinked. "Maybe tomorrow we should go out and take a look."

Twilight and Digger alighted at that moment next to them on the branch.

"Take a look?" Digger asked. "A look for what?"

"Ezylryb," Twilight said. "I heard them talking too."

There was a sudden pulsing of light in the sky and then a gasp from all the owls as a radiance swept the black night.

"What is it? What is it?"

"Oh, great Glaux, we are blessed!" hooted Barran.

"It is the Aurora Glaucora," Boron sang out.

Soren, Gylfie, Digger, Twilight and Eglantine all looked at one another. They had no idea what Barran and Boron were talking about. But the sky seemed rinsed with colours, colours that streamed like banners through the night. Suddenly, Madame Plonk abandoned her perch by the harp and flew out into the brilliance of the night. Still singing, she swept through the long lances of light, her white body reflecting the colours. It was irresistible. Soren remembered that morning months ago when he and Madame Plonk had flown through the rainbow. But the rainbow was pale next to these pulsing banners of light that draped the sky.

His worries about Ezylryb grew dimmer as the colours grew brighter. The sky beckoned, the shimmering light drew them. But there was a strangeness to it all. He felt a shudder deep in his gizzard. Behind those banners of throbbing light he knew there was blackness. Ezylryb was still missing, St Aggie's was still a threat, and now there was the almost unthinkable, the nearly unspeakable 'you only wish'. Yes, Eglantine was back, but was she really back? Was it the same dear Eglantine? Soren felt as if he could no longer trust. For the world on this night had suddenly become too strange. It was as if everything had been turned inside out and the thing that owls called heaven, glaumora, had come down to Earth and swallowed the night. But this was not quite right, Soren thought. Just at that moment Eglantine swept in beside her brother.

"Isn't it beautiful, Soren? Isn't it just beautiful?"

"Just beautiful," Soren said absently.

But even as he spoke, he felt a strange dread in his gizzard. *Well*, he finally thought, *Eglantine and I are together at last, and we need no colours, for just flying with her at my side is as good as glaumora on Earth. Tomorrow, yes tomorrow, I shall search for Ezylryb.* Soren recalled the amber squint of the old Whiskered Screech's injured eye that indeed sparkled with the glint of deepest knowledge. But tonight... Soren and Eglantine tipped their white faces to the tinted sky and flew off into the painted night just as the Golden Talons began to rise.

And yet the talons were no longer golden, just as the sky was no longer black.

THE OWLS
and others from Guardians of Ga'Hoole

The Capture

SOREN: Barn Owl, *Tyto alba,* from the kingdom of the Forest of Tyto; snatched when he was three weeks old by St Aegolius patrols; escaped from St Aegolius Academy for Orphan Owls

His family:

KLUDD: Barn Owl, *Tyto alba,* older brother

EGLANTINE: Barn Owl, *Tyto alba,* younger sister

NOCTUS: Barn Owl, *Tyto alba,* father

MARILLA: Barn Owl, *Tyto alba,* mother

His family's nest-maid:
MRS PLITHIVER: blind snake

GYLFIE: Elf Owl, *Micrathene whitneyi,* from the desert kingdom of Kuneer; snatched when she was three weeks old by St

Aegolius patrols; escaped from St Aegolius Academy for Orphan Owls; Soren's best friend

TWILIGHT: Great Grey Owl, *Strix nebulosa,* free flyer, orphaned within hours of hatching

DIGGER: Burrowing Owl, *Speotyto cunicularius,* from the desert kingdom of Kuneer; lost in desert after attack in which his brother was killed and eaten by owls from St Aegolius

BORON: Snowy Owl, *Nyctea scandiaca,* the king of Hoole

BARRAN: Snowy Owl, *Nyctea scandiaca,* the queen of Hoole

MATRON: Short-eared Owl, *Asio flammeus,* the motherly caretaker at the Great Ga'Hoole Tree

STRIX STRUMA: Spotted Owl, *Strix occidentalis,* the dignified navigation ryb (teacher) at the Great Ga'Hoole Tree

ELVAN:	Great Grey Owl, *Strix nebulosa,* the colliering ryb (teacher) at the Great Ga'Hoole Tree
EZYLRYB:	Whiskered Screech Owl, *Otus trichopsis,* the wise weather-interpretation ryb (teacher) at the Great Ga'Hoole Tree; Soren's mentor
POOT:	Boreal Owl, *Aegolius funerus,* Ezylryb's assistant
BUBO:	Great Horned Owl, *Bubo virginianus,* the blacksmith of the Great Ga'Hoole Tree
MADAME PLONK:	Snowy Owl, *Nyctea scandiaca,* the elegant singer of the Great Ga'Hoole Tree
OCTAVIA:	Madame Plonk's blind nest-maid snake
TRADER MAGS:	Magpie, a travelling merchant
OTULISSA:	Spotted Owl, *Strix occidentalis,* a student of prestigious lineage at the Great Ga'Hoole Tree

PRIMROSE: Pygmy Owl, *Glaucidium gnoma,* rescued from a forest fire and brought to the Great Ga'Hoole Tree the night of Soren and his friends' arrival

MARTIN: Northern Saw-whet Owl, *Aegolius acadicus,* rescued and brought to the Great Ga'Hoole Tree the same night as Primrose

RUBY: Short-eared Owl, *Asio flammeus;* lost her family under mysterious circumstances and was brought to the Great Ga'Hoole Tree.

The Legend takes flight again...

Read a sneak preview of the next book
in the Guardians of Ga'Hoole series,

The Rescue

Soren, as he glanced around, found the forest quite strange. All the trees were white-barked and not one had a single leaf. Indeed, although it was night, this forest had a kind of luminance that made the moon pale by comparison.

"I would guess," said Otulissa as she studied the sky, "that we are between rain bands here."

Poot looked around uneasily. "That or a spirit woods."

A chill ran through them all. "A spirit woods?" Martin said softly. "I've heard of them."

"Yeah, you've heard of them. You don't necessarily want to spend the night in them," Poot replied.

"I don't know, Poot," Ruby spoke in a nervous low voice, "whether we've got much choice. I mean that hurricane's still going. I've seen the worst of it. It's not something you want to mess with."

"What are we gonna do, Poot?" Silver asked, a slight tremor in his voice.

"Not much choice, as Ruby said. Just hope we don't disturb any scrooms."

"Scrooms!" Nut Beam and Silver wailed.

"Well, I don't believe in them," Martin said and stomped his small talons into the moss-covered ground. Then, as if to prove it, he lifted off and began to search for a tree to light down in.

"You mind what tree you choose. You don't want to disturb a scroom," Poot called after him. But Soren thought that maybe after having been sucked up in a rain band, then dropped into the sea, a scroom was nothing to Martin.

Scrooms were disembodied spirits of owls who had died and had not quite made it all the way to glaumora, which was the special owl heaven where the souls of owls went. Nut Beam and Silver, however, had begun to cry uncontrollably.

"Pull yourselves together, both of you," Otulissa exploded angrily. "There's no such thing as scrooms. An atmospheric disturbance. False light. That's all. Strix Emerilla has written about it in a very erudite book entitled *Spectroscopic Anomalies: Shifts in Shape and Light.*"

"Yes, there are scrooms!" the two owlets hooted back shrilly.

"My grandma said so," Nut Beam said defiantly and stomped a small talon on the moss.

"I've heard enough about your grandmas," Otulissa snapped. "Poot, how long do we have to stay here?"

"Until the hurricane blows through. Can't take these young'uns" – he nodded towards Silver and Nut Beam – "out in this. Too inexperienced."

"You're making us stay here – with scrooms?" Nut Beam protested. And as if on cue, Silver started to wail again.

"I think we need to organise a hunting party," Otulissa said.

"Yes, yes, immediately," Poot said. He began to flutter about the group. "Now, there's no telling what one can find in such a woods."

It was obvious to Soren, Ruby and Martin that Otulissa had embarrassed Poot, who might be a terrific flier but not a natural leader. They felt the absence of Ezylryb more than ever.

But then Poot seemed to be jarred into action. He swelled up with authority and tried his best to sound like a leader. "Soren," Poot said, "you and Ruby can cover the northeast quadrant of this woods. You fly it hard now, young'uns. We got some hungry beaks here. Martin and Otulissa can cover the southwest one. I'll stay here with the young'uns."

"Ha!" Ruby gave a harsh sound and ascended through the branches. "I think Poot's scared of scrooms. That's why he sent us out. You scared, Soren?" They had gained some altitude now and the strange mist that floated through the white trees below seemed to evaporate.

"Sort of," Soren said.

"Well, at least you're honest. But what do you mean by 'sort of'?"

"I think the idea of a scroom is not so much scary as sad. I mean scrooms are supposed to be spirits that didn't quite make it to glaumora. That's kind of sad."

"I suppose so," Ruby said.

Suppose so? Soren blinked at Ruby. He thought it was terribly sad, but Ruby wasn't the deepest owl. She was a fantastic flier and a great chaw mate and lots of fun but, although she felt things in her gizzard like all owls, she was not given to reflecting deeply. But now she surprised him. "How come they don't make it to glaumora?"

"I'm not sure. Mrs P said that it was because they might have unfinished business on earth."

"Mrs Plithiver? How would she know? She's a snake."

"I sometimes think that Mrs P knows more about owls than owls do." Soren cocked his head suddenly. "Sssh." Ruby shut her beak immediately. She, like all other owls, had great respect for the extraordinary hearing abilities of Barn Owls. "Ground squirrel below."

There were actually three in all. And Ruby, who was incredibly fast with her talons, managed to get two in one single slicing swipe. They were more successful than Martin and Otulissa, who had only come back with two very small mice.

By the time they had finished eating, the night was thinning into day. Although with the mist that seemed to wrap itself through the branches of the white-barked trees, Soren thought that it seemed like twilight in these woods.

"I think," Poot announced, "it's time for us to turn in. Not for a full day's sleep, mind you. We'll leave before First Black. No fear of crows around here." He slid his neck about in a slow twist as if scanning the wood.

"No. Just scrooms," Nut Beam said.

"Nut Beam, shut your beak," Martin screeched fiercely.

"Now, now, Martin! Don't like that tone, lad," Poot said, trying to sound very—

Very what? wondered Soren. *Like Ezylryb? Never like the Captain.*

"Well, I've been doing some thinking," Poot went on to say. "And I think that this being a spirit woods as some calls 'em, I think it's best that we keep to the ground for sleeping, no perching in them trees." He swivelled his head around in a slow sweeping movement, as if he were almost trying to push back the bone-white trees that surrounded them.

A hush fell upon the group. Soren thought he could hear the beat of their hearts quicken. *This scroom stuff must really be serious,* he said to himself. Even Ruby looked a little nervous. For an owl to sleep on the ground was almost unheard of, unless, of course, it was a Burrowing Owl who lived in the desert, like Digger. There were dangers on the ground. Predators – like raccoons.

"I know what you be thinking," Poot continued nervously and seemed to avoid looking them in the eye as Ezylryb would have. "I know you're thinking that for an owl to ground sleep ain't natural. But these ain't natural woods. And it's said that these trees might really belong to the scrooms. You never know which one a scroom might light down in and it's best to leave the trees be. I'm older than you young'uns. Got more experience. And I'd be daft not to tell you that my gizzard is giving me some mighty twinges."

"Mine, too!" said Silver.

"Probably has a gizzard the size of a pea," Martin whispered.

"Now don'cha go worry too much. We just got to be vigi-ful," Poot continued.

"You mean 'vigilant'?" Otulissa said.

"Don't smart beak me, lassie. We's gonna set up a watch. I'll take the first one with Martin. Otulissa and Ruby you take the next. And Soren you take the last. You have to do it alone, but it be the shortest one, lad. So nothin' to fear."

Nothing to fear? Then why doesn't he take it? Soren thought, but he knew that the one thing a chaw owl never did was question a command. All of the owls turned their heads towards Soren.

Martin stepped forwards. "I'll stay up with you, Soren."

Soren blinked at the little Northern Saw-whet. "No, no – that's very kind of you, Martin, but you'll be tired. You must already be tired. I mean you've fallen into the sea. Don't worry, Martin. I'll be fine."

"No, Soren, I mean it."

"No, I'll be fine," Soren said firmly.

The truth was that during that first watch they were all too nervous to sleep and the ground was a terrible place to even try to sleep to begin with. But as the dark faded and the white of the trees melted into the lightness of the morning, they did grow sleepier and sleepier. The owls' heads began to droop lower and lower until they were resting on their breasts or on their backs, as it was the habit of very young owls to twist their heads around and rest them just between their shoulders.

*   *   *

"Your watch, Soren," Ruby said.

His eyes blinked open. He lifted his head.

"Don't worry. There is nothing out here. Not a raccoon, not a scroom, not a scroom of a raccoon." Otulissa churred softly, which was the sound that owls made when they laughed.

Soren walked over to the watch mound that was in a small clearing. He spread his wings and, in one brief upstroke, rose to settle on the top of the mound. The fog in the forest had thickened again. A soft breeze swirled through the woods, stirring and spinning the mist into fluffy shapes. Some of the mist clouds were long and skinny, others puffy. Soren thought of the silly jabber of the young owlets when they had been flying earlier, before encountering the hurricane. The owlets were sort of cute, he guessed, in their own annoying little way. It was hard to believe, however, that he had ever been that young. He had barely known his parents before he had been snatched, and he had never known his grandparents. There had been no time. He blinked his eyes at the mist that was now whirling into new shapes. It was strange how one could start to read this ground mist like clouds, find pictures in them – a raccoon, a deer bounding over a tree stump, a fish leaping from a river. Soren had tried sometimes to make up stories about cloud pictures when he was flying. The vapours just ahead of him had clumped together into one large shapeless mass, but now they seemed to be pulling apart again into two clumps. There was something vaguely familiar about the shapes that these clumps were becoming. What was it? A lovely downy bundle that looked so soft and warm. Something seemed to call to him and yet there was no sound. How could that be?

Soren grew very still. Something was happening. He was not frightened. No, not frightened at all. But sad, yes, deeply and terribly sad. He felt himself drawn to these two shapes. They were fluffy and their heads were cocked in such a familiar way as if they were listening to him. And they were calling to him, and they were saying things but there were no sounds. It was as if the voices were sealed inside his head. Just then, he felt himself step out of his body. He felt his wings spread. He was lifting, and yet he was still there on the mound. He could see his talons planted on the mossy top with the tangle of ivy. But, at the same time, he could see something moving out of him. It was him – but not him. It was his shape, pale and misty and swirling like the other shapes. The thing that was him but not him was lifting, rising, and spreading its wings in flight to perch in the big white tree at the edge of the clearing where the two other misty figures perched.

False light?

No, not false light, Soren.

Scrooms?

If you must.

Mum? Da?

About the Author

Kathryn Lasky has long had a fascination with owls. Several years ago she began doing research into these birds and their behaviour – what they ate, how they flew, how they built their nests – with a view to writing a nonfiction book about owls, illustrated with photographs by her husband. She realised, though, that this would be difficult since owls are nocturnal creatures, shy and hard to find. So she decided to write a fantasy about a world of owls instead, and include as much real natural history as she could.

Kathryn Lasky and her husband live in Cambridge, Massachusetts.